"Many science fiction anthologies are published every year, but you rarely find one with more than a couple of good stories in it. This book is an exception. You could not expect less when you have Robert Silverberg as editor and such authors as Robert A. Heinlein, R. A. Lafferty and Arthur C. Clarke."

— *The Portland Oregon Journal*

OTHER DIMENSIONS

Edited by Robert Silverberg

PINNACLE BOOKS • NEW YORK CITY

OTHER DIMENSIONS

Copyright © 1973 by Robert Silverberg

A Pinnacle book, published by special arrangement with
Hawthorn Books, Inc., New York.

ISBN: 0-523-00422-2

First printing, September 1974

Printed in the United States of America

PINNACLE BOOKS, INC.
275 Madison Avenue
New York, N.Y.

Acknowledgments

Contents

INTRODUCTION

A dimension, according to the *Oxford English Dictionary*, is "a mode of linear measurement, or extension, in a particular direction." No one could quarrel with that definition, least of all a science-fiction writer. To him, a dimension is a mode of extension in a very particular direction: that of wonder and strangeness. Not merely the much-discussed fourth dimension, but fifth, sixth, and infinite dimensions, fall into the province of science fiction, along with a few dimensions that are impossible to locate along any conceivable axis of the space-time continuum.

The stories in this book illustrate the range of science fiction's fascination with other dimensions. Several of them are serious-minded explorations of the geometrical intricacies of four-dimensional solids. One deals with a two-dimensional world. A number of them examine the worlds that lie alongside ours, or other tracks in time. A couple are amiable spoofs, flickering in and out of space and time in a spirit of high good humor. No special mathematical knowledge is needed to enjoy any of them—although the probability is high that the reader will come away from this book with a deeper understanding of the concept of dimensions than he had before.

ROBERT SILVERBERG

OTHER
DIMENSIONS

—And He Built a Crooked House

ROBERT A. HEINLEIN

More than any other writer since H. G. Wells, Robert A. Heinlein has been responsible for giving form and direction to science fiction. From such early novels as *Beyond This Horizon* and *Methuselah's Children* of the 1940's to *Stranger in a Strange Land* and *The Moon Is a Harsh Mistress* in the 1960's, Heinlein has shaped, defined, and expanded the nature of the science-fiction story. One technique basic to the Heinlein approach is to choose a speculative theme and push it to its ultimate implications, wringing every possible imaginative consequence from it along the way. This he did to hilarious effect in the story here, dating from 1940 but not dated at all, of the four-dimensional house.

Americans are considered crazy anywhere in the world.

They will usually concede a basis for the accusation but point to California as the focus of the infection. Californians stoutly maintain that their bad reputation is derived solely from the acts of the inhabitants of Los Angeles County. Angelenos will, when pressed, admit the charge but explain hastily, "It's Hollywood. It's not our fault—we didn't ask for it; Hollywood just grew."

The people in Hollywood don't care; they glory in it. If you are interested, they will drive you up Laurel Canyon

3

"where we keep the violent cases." The Canyonites—the brown-legged women, the trunks-clad men constantly busy building and rebuilding their slaphappy unfinished houses—regard with faint contempt the dull creatures who live down in the flats, and treasure in their hearts the secret knowledge that they, and only they, know how to live.

Lookout Mountain Avenue is the name of a side canyon which twists up from Laurel Canyon. The other Canyonites don't like to have it mentioned; after all, one must draw the line somewhere!

High up on Lookout Mountain at Number 8775, across the street from the Hermit—the original Hermit of Hollywood—lived Quintus Teal, graduate architect.

Even the architecture of southern California is different. Hot dogs are sold from a structure built like and designated "The Pup." Ice-cream cones come from a giant stucco ice-cream cone, and neon proclaims, "Get the Chili Bowl Habit!" from the roofs of buildings which are indisputably chili bowls. Gasoline, oil, and free road maps are dispensed beneath the wings of trimotored transport planes, while the certified rest rooms, inspected hourly for your comfort, are located in the cabin of the plane itself. These things may surprise, or amuse, the tourist, but the local residents, who walk bareheaded in the famous California noonday sun, take them as a matter of course.

Quintus Teal regarded the efforts of his colleagues in architecture as fainthearted, fumbling, and timid.

"What is a house?" Teal demanded of his friend, Homer Bailey.

"Well—" Bailey admitted cautiously—"speaking in broad terms, I've always regarded a house as a gadget to keep off the rain."

"Nuts! You're as bad as the rest of them."

"I didn't say the definition was complete——"

"Complete! It isn't even in the right direction. From

that point of view we might just as well be squatting in caves. But I don't blame you," Teal went on magnanimously, "you're no worse than the lugs you find practicing architecture. Even the Moderns—all they've done is to abandon the Wedding Cake School in favor of the Service Station School, chucked away the gingerbread and slapped on some chromium, but at heart they are as conservative and traditional as a county courthouse. Neutra! Schindler! What have those bums got? What's Frank Lloyd Wright got that I haven't got?"

"Commissions," his friend answered succinctly.

"Huh? Wha' d'ju say?" Teal stumbled slightly in his flow of words, did a slight double take, and recovered himself. "Commissions. Correct. And why? Because I don't think of a house as an upholstered cave; I think of it as a machine for living, a vital process, a live dynamic thing, changing with the mood of the dweller—not a dead, static, oversized coffin. Why should we be held down by the frozen concepts of our ancestors? Any fool with a little smattering of descriptive geometry can design a house in the ordinary way. Is the static geometry of Euclid the only mathematics? Are we to completely disregard the Picard-Vessiot theory? How about modular systems? To say nothing of the rich suggestions of stereochemistry. Isn't there a place in architecture for transformation, for homomorphology, for actional structures?"

"Blessed if I know," answered Bailey. "You might just as well be talking about the fourth dimension for all it means to me."

"And why not? Why should we limit ourselves to the— Say!" He interrupted himself and stared into distances. "Homer, I think you've really got something. After all, why not? Think of the infinite richness of articulation and relationship in four dimensions. What a house, what a house—" He stood quite still, his pale bulging eyes blinking thoughtfully.

Bailey reached up and shook his arm. "Snap out of it. What the hell are you talking about, four dimensions? Time is the fourth dimension; you can't drive nails into *that*."

Teal shrugged him off. "Sure. Sure. Time is a fourth dimension, but I'm thinking about a fourth spatial dimension, like length, breadth, and thickness. For economy of materials and convenience of arrangement you couldn't beat it. To say nothing of the saving of ground space— you could put an eight-room house on the land now occupied by a one-room house. Like a tesseract——"

"What's a tesseract?"

"Didn't you go to school? A tesseract is a hypercube, a square figure with four dimensions to it, like a cube has three, and a square has two. Here, I'll show you." Teal dashed out into the kitchen of his apartment and returned with a box of toothpicks, which he spilled on the table between them, brushing glasses and a nearly empty Holland gin bottle carelessly aside. "I'll need some plasticine. I had some around here last week." He burrowed into a drawer of the littered desk which crowded one corner of his dining room and emerged with a lump of oily sculptor's clay. "Here's some."

"What are you going to do?"

"I'll show you." Teal rapidly pinched off small masses of the clay and rolled them into pea-sized balls. He stuck toothpicks into four of these and hooked them together into a square. "There! That's a square."

"Obviously."

"Another one like it, four more toothpicks, and we make a cube." The toothpicks were now arranged in the framework of a square box, a cube, with the pellets of clay holding the corners together. "Now we make another cube just like the first one, and the two of them will be two sides of the tesseract."

Bailey started to help him roll the little balls of clay for the second cube, but became diverted by the sensuous feel of the docile clay and started working and shaping it with his fingers.

"Look," he said, holding up his effort, a tiny figurine, "Gypsy Rose Lee."

"Looks more like Gargantua; she ought to sue you. Now pay attention. You open up one corner of the first cube, interlock the second cube at one corner, and then close the corner. Then take eight more toothpicks and join the bottom of the first cube to the bottom of the second, on a slant, and the top of the first to the top of the second, the same way." This he did rapidly while he talked.

"What's that supposed to be?" Bailey demanded suspiciously.

"That's a tesseract, eight cubes forming the sides of a hypercube in four dimensions."

"It looks more like a cat's cradle to me. You've only got two cubes there anyhow. Where are the other six?"

"Use your imagination, man. Consider the top of the first cube in relation to the top of the second; that's cube number three. Then the two bottom squares, then the front faces of each cube, the back faces, the right hand, the left hand—eight cubes." He pointed them out.

"Yeah, I see 'em. But they still aren't cubes; they're watchamacallems—prisms. They are not square; they slant."

"That's just the way you look at it, in perspective. If you drew a picture of a cube on a piece of paper, the side squares would be slaunchwise, wouldn't they? That's perspective. When you look at a four-dimensional figure in three dimensions, naturally it looks crooked. But those are all cubes just the same."

"Maybe they are to you, brother, but they still look crooked to me."

Teal ignored the objections and went on. "Now consider this as the framework of an eight-room house; there's one room on the ground floor—that's for service, utilities, and garage. There are six rooms opening off it on the next floor, living room, dining room, bath, bedrooms, and so forth. And up at the top, completely enclosed and with windows on four sides, is your study. There! How do you like it?"

"Seems to me you have the bathtub hanging out of the living-room ceiling. Those rooms are interlaced like an octopus."

"Only in perspective, only in perspective. Here, I'll do it another way so you can see it." This time Teal made a cube of toothpicks, then made a second of halves of toothpicks, and set it exactly in the center of the first by attaching the corners of the small cube to the large cube by short lengths of toothpick. "Now—the big cube is your ground floor; the little cube inside is your study on the top floor. The six cubes joining them are the living rooms. See?"

Bailey studied the figure, then shook his head. "I still don't see but two cubes, a big one and a little one. Those other six things, they look like pyramids this time instead of prisms, but they aren't cubes."

"Certainly, certainly, you are seeing them in different perspective. Can't you see that?"

"Well, maybe. But that room on the inside, there. It's completely surrounded by the thingamajigs. I thought you said it had windows on four sides."

"It has—it just looks like it is surrounded. That's the grand feature about a tesseract house, complete outside exposure for every room, yet every wall serves two rooms and an eight-room house requires only a one-room foundation. It's revolutionary."

"That's putting it mildly. You're crazy, bud; you can't build a house like that. That inside room is on the inside, and there she stays."

Teal looked at his friend in controlled exasperation. "It's

guys like you that keep architecture in its infancy. How many square sides has a cube?"

"Six."

"How many of them are inside?"

"Why, none of 'em. They're all on the outside."

"All right. Now listen—a tesseract has eight cubical sides, *all on the outside*. Now watch me. I'm going to open up this tesseract like you can open up a cubical pasteboard box, until it's flat. That way you'll be able to see all eight of the cubes." Working very rapidly he constructed four cubes, piling one on top of the other in an unsteady tower. He then built out four more cubes from the four exposed faces of the second cube in the pile. The structure swayed a little under the loose coupling of the clay pellets, but it stood, eight cubes in an inverted cross, a double cross, as the four additional cubes stuck out in four directions. "Do you see it now? It rests on the ground-floor room, the next six cubes are the living rooms, and there is your study, up at the top."

Bailey regarded it with more approval than he had the other figures. "At least I can understand it. You say that is a tesseract, too?"

"That is a tesseract unfolded in three dimensions. To put it back together you tuck the top cube onto the bottom cube, fold those side cubes in till they meet the top cube, and there you are. You do all this folding through a fourth dimension of course; you don't distort any of the cubes or fold them into each other."

Bailey studied the wobbly framework further. "Look here," he said at last, "why don't you forget about folding this thing up through a fourth dimension—you can't anyway—and build a house like this?"

"What do you mean, I can't? It's a simple mathematical problem——"

"Take it easy, son. It may be simple in mathematics, but you could never get your plans approved for construction. There isn't any fourth dimension; forget it. But this kind of a house—it might have some advantages."

Checked, Teal studied the model. "Hm-m-m—maybe you got something. We could have the same number of rooms, and we'd save the same amount of ground space. Yes, and we would set that middle cross-shaped floor northeast, southwest, and so forth, so that every room would get sunlight all day long. That central axis lends itself nicely to central heating. We'll put the dining room on the northeast and the kitchen on the southeast, with big view windows in every room. Okay, Homer, I'll do it! Where do you want it built?"

"Wait a minute! Wait a minute! I didn't say you were going to build it for me——"

"Of course I am. Who else? Your wife wants a new house; this is it."

"But Mrs. Bailey wants a Georgian house——"

"Just an idea she had. Women don't know what they want——"

"Mrs. Bailey does."

"Just some idea an out-of-date architect has put in her head. She drives a 1941 car, doesn't she? She wears the very latest styles—why should she live in an eighteenth-century house? This house will be even later than a 1941 model; it's years in the future. She'll be the talk of the town."

"Well—I'll have to talk to her."

"Nothing of the sort. We'll surprise her with it. Have another drink."

"Anyhow, we can't do anything about it now. Mrs. Bailey and I are driving up to Bakersfield tomorrow. The company's bringing in a couple of wells tomorrow."

"Nonsense. That's just the opportunity we want. It will be a surprise for her when you get back. You can just write me a check right now, and your worries are over."

"I oughtn't to do anything like this without consulting her. She won't like it."

"Say, who wears the pants in your family anyhow?"

The check was signed about halfway down the second bottle.

Things are done fast in southern California. Ordinary houses there are usually built in a month's time. Under Teal's impassioned heckling the tesseract house climbed dizzily skyward in days rather than weeks, and its cross-shaped second story came jutting out at the four corners of the world. He had some trouble at first with the inspectors over these four projecting rooms, but by using strong girders and folding money he had been able to convince them of the soundness of his engineering.

By arrangement, Teal drove up in front of the Bailey residence the morning after their return to town. He improvised on his two-tone horn. Bailey stuck his head out the front door. "Why don't you use the bell?"

"Too slow," answered Teal cheerfully. "I'm a man of action. Is Mrs. Bailey ready? Ah, there you are, Mrs. Bailey! Welcome home, welcome home. Jump in, we've got a surprise for you!"

"You know Teal, my dear," Bailey put in uncomfortably.

Mrs. Bailey sniffed. "I know him. We'll go in our own car, Homer."

"Certainly, my dear."

"Good idea," Teal agreed; " 'sgot more power than mine; we'll get there faster. I'll drive, I know the way." He took the keys from Bailey, slid into the driver's seat, and had the engine started before Mrs. Bailey could rally her forces.

"Never have to worry about my driving," he assured Mrs. Bailey, turning his head as he did so, while he shot the powerful car down the avenue and swung onto Sunset Boulevard; "it's a matter of power and control, a dynamic process, just my meat—I've never had a serious accident."

"You won't have but one," she said bitingly. "Will you *please* keep your eyes on the traffic?"

He attempted to explain to her that a traffic situation

was a matter, not of eyesight, but intuitive integration of courses, speeds, and probabilities, but Bailey cut him short. "Where is the house, Quintus?"

"House?" asked Mrs. Bailey suspiciously. "What's this about a house, Homer? Have you been up to something without telling me?"

Teal cut in with his best diplomatic manner. "It certainly is a house, Mrs. Bailey. And what a house! It's a surprise for you from a devoted husband. Just wait till you see it——"

"I shall," she agreed grimly. "What style is it?"

"This house sets a new style. It's later than television, newer than next week. It must be seen to be appreciated. By the way," he went on rapidly, heading off any retort, "did you folks feel the earthquake last night?"

"Earthquake? What earthquake? Homer, was there an earthquake?"

"Just a little one," Teal continued, "about two A.M. If I hadn't been awake, I wouldn't have noticed it."

Mrs. Bailey shuddered. "Oh, this awful country! Do you hear that, Homer? We might have been killed in our beds and never have known it. Why did I ever let you persuade me to leave Iowa?"

"But, my dear," he protested hopelessly, "you wanted to come out to California; you didn't like Des Moines."

"We needn't go into that," she said firmly. "You are a man; you should anticipate such things. Earthquakes!"

"That's one thing you needn't fear in your new home, Mrs. Bailey," Teal told her. "It's absolutely earthquake-proof; every part is in perfect dynamic balance with every other part."

"Well, I hope so. Where is this house?"

"Just around this bend. There's the sign now." A large arrow sign, of the sort favored by real-estate promoters, proclaimed in letters that were large and bright even for southern California:

THE HOUSE OF THE FUTURE!!!

COLOSSAL—AMAZING—REVOLUTIONARY

See how your grandchildren will live!

Q. Teal, Architect

"Of course that will be taken down," he added hastily, noting her expression, "as soon as you take possession." He slued around the corner and brought the car to a squealing halt in front of the House of the Future. *"Voila!"* He watched their faces for response.

Bailey stared unbelievingly, Mrs. Bailey in open dislike. They saw a simple cubical mass, possessing doors and windows, but no other architectural features, save that it was decorated in intricate mathematical designs. "Teal," Bailey asked slowly, "what have you been up to?"

Teal turned from their faces to the house. Gone was the crazy tower with its jutting second-story rooms. No trace remained of the seven rooms above ground-floor level. Nothing remained but the single room that rested on the foundations. "Great jumping cats!" he yelled. "I've been robbed!"

He broke into a run.

But it did him no good. Front or back, the story was the same: the other seven rooms had disappeared, vanished completely. Bailey caught up with him and took his arm.

"Explain yourself. What is this about being robbed? How come you built anything like this—it's not according to agreement."

"But I didn't. I built just what we had planned to build, an eight-room house in the form of a developed tesseract. I've been sabotaged; that's what it is! Jealousy! The other architects in town didn't dare let me finish this job; they knew they'd be washed up if I did."

"When were you last here?"

"Yesterday afternoon."

"Everything all right then?"

"Yes. The gardeners were just finishing up."

Bailey glanced around at the faultlessly manicured landscaping. "I don't see how seven rooms could have been dismantled and carted away from here in a single night without wrecking this garden."

Teal looked around, too. "It doesn't look it. I don't understand it."

Mrs. Bailey joined them. "Well? Well? Am I to be left to amuse myself? We might as well look it over as long as we are here, though I'm warning you, Homer, I'm not going to like it."

"We might as well," agreed Teal and drew a key from his pocket with which he let them in the front door. "We may pick up some clues."

The entrance hall was in perfect order; the sliding screens that separated it from the garage space were back, permitting them to see the entire compartment. "This looks all right," observed Bailey. "Let's go up on the roof and try to figure out what happened. Where's the staircase? Have they stolen that, too?"

"Oh, no," Teal denied, "look—" He pressed a button below the light switch; a panel in the ceiling fell away, and a light, graceful flight of stairs swung noiselessly down. Its strength members were the frosty silver of Duralumin, its treads and risers transparent plastic. Teal wriggled like a boy who has successfully performed a card trick while Mrs. Bailey thawed perceptibly.

It was beautiful.

"Pretty slick," Bailey admitted. "Howsomever it doesn't seem to go anyplace——"

"Oh, that—" Teal followed his gaze. "The cover lifts up as you approach the top. Open stairwells are anachronisms. Come on." As predicted, the lid of the staircase got out of their way as they climbed the flight and permitted them to debouch at the top, but not, as they had expected, on the roof of the single room. They found themselves standing in the middle one of the five rooms which constituted the second floor of the original structure.

For the first time on record Teal had nothing to say. Bailey echoed him, chewing on his cigar. Everything was in perfect order. Before them, through open doorway and translucent partition, lay the kitchen, a chef's dream of up-to-the-minute domestic engineering, Monel metal, continuous counter space, concealed lighting, functional arrangement. On the left the formal, yet gracious and hospitable, dining room awaited guests, its furniture in parade-ground alignment.

Teal knew before he turned his head that the drawing room and lounge would be found in equally substantial and impossible existence.

"Well, I must admit this *is* charming," Mrs. Bailey approved, "and the kitchen is just *too* quaint for words—though I would never have guessed from the exterior that this house had so much room upstairs. Of course *some* changes will have to be made. That secretary now—if we moved it over *here* and put the settle over *there*——"

"Stow it, Matilda," Bailey cut in brusquely. "What d'yuh make of it, Teal?"

"Why, Homer Bailey! The very id——"

"Stow it, I said. Well, Teal?"

The architect shuffled his rambling body. "I'm afraid to say. Let's go on up."

"How?"

"Like this." He touched another button; a mate, in deeper colors, to the fairy bridge that had let them up from below offered them access to the next floor. They climbed it, Mrs. Bailey expostulating in the rear, and found themselves in the master bedroom. Its shades were drawn, as had been those on the level below, but the mellow lighting came on automatically. Teal at once activated the switch which controlled still another flight of stairs, and they hurried up into the top-floor study.

"Look, Teal," suggested Bailey when he had caught his breath, "can we get to the roof above this room? Then we could look around."

"Sure, it's an observatory platform." They climbed a fourth flight of stairs, but when the cover at the top lifted to let them reach the level above, they found themselves, not on the roof, but *standing in the ground-floor room where they had entered the house.*

Mr. Bailey turned a sickly gray. "Angels in heaven," he cried, "this place is haunted. We're getting out of here." Grabbing his wife, he threw open the front door and plunged out.

Teal was too much preoccupied to bother with their departure. There was an answer to all this, an answer that he did not believe. But he was forced to break off considering it because of hoarse shouts from somewhere above him. He lowered the staircase and rushed upstairs. Bailey was in the central room leaning over Mrs. Bailey, who had fainted. Teal took in the situation, went to the bar built into the lounge, and poured three fingers of brandy, which he returned with and handed to Bailey. "Here—this'll fix her up."

Bailey drank it.

"That was for Mrs. Bailey," said Teal.

"Don't quibble," snapped Bailey. "Get her another." Teal took the precaution of taking one himself before returning with a dose earmarked for his client's wife. He found her just opening her eyes.

"Here, Mrs. Bailey," he soothed, "this will make you feel better."

"I never touch spirits," she protested and gulped it.

"Now tell me what happened," suggested Teal. "I thought you two had left."

"But we did—we walked out the front door and found ourselves up here, in the lounge."

"The hell you say! Hm-m-m—wait a minute." Teal went into the lounge. There he found that the big view window at the end of the room was open. He peered cautiously through it. He stared, not out at the California countryside, but into the ground-floor room—or a reasonable facsimile thereof. He said nothing, but went back to the stairwell, which he had left open, and looked down it. The ground-floor room was still in place. Somehow, it managed to be in two different places at once, on different levels.

He came back into the central room and seated himself opposite Bailey in a deep, low chair and sighted him past his upthrust bony knees. "Homer," he said impressively, "do you know what has happened?"

"No, I don't—but if I don't find out pretty soon, something is going to happen and pretty drastic, too!"

"Homer, this is a vindication of my theories. This house is a real tesseract."

"What's he talking about, Homer?"

"Wait, Matilda—now Teal, that's ridiculous. You've pulled some hanky-panky here and I won't have it—scaring Mrs. Bailey half to death, and making me nervous. All I want is to get out of here, with no more of your trapdoors and silly practical jokes."

"Speak for yourself, Homer," Mrs. Bailey interrupted. "I was *not* frightened; I was just took all over queer for a moment. It's my heart; all of my people are delicate and highstrung. Now about this tessy thing—explain yourself, Mr. Teal. Speak up."

He told her as well as he could in the face of numerous interruptions the theory back of the house. "Now as I see it, Mrs. Bailey," he concluded, "this house, while perfectly stable in three dimensions, was not stable in four dimensions. I had built a house in the shape of an unfolded tesseract; something happened to it, some jar or side thrust, and it collapsed into its normal shape—it folded up." He snapped his fingers suddenly. "I've got it! The earthquake!"

"Earthquake?"

"Yes, yes, the little shake we had last night. From a four-dimensional standpoint this house was like a plane balanced on edge. One little push and it fell over, collapsed along its natural joints into a stable four-dimensional figure."

"I thought you boasted about how safe this house was."

"It is safe—three-dimensionally."

"I don't call a house safe," commented Bailey edgily, "that collapses at the first little tremblor."

"But look around you, man!" Teal protested. "Nothing has been disturbed, not a piece of glassware cracked. Rotation through a fourth dimension can't affect a three-dimensional figure any more than you can shake letters off a printed page. If you had been sleeping in here last night, you would never have awakened."

"That's just what I'm afraid of. Incidentally, has your great genius figured out any way for us to get out of this booby trap?"

"Huh? Oh, yes, you and Mrs. Bailey started to leave and landed back up here, didn't you? But I'm sure there is no real difficulty—we came in; we can go out. I'll try it." He was up and hurrying downstairs before he had finished talking. He flung open the front door, stepped through, and found himself staring at his companions, down the length of the second-floor lounge. "Well, there does seem to be some slight problem," he admitted blandly. "A mere technicality, though—we can always go out a window." He jerked aside the long drapes that covered the deep French windows set in one side wall of the lounge. He stopped suddenly.

"Hm-m-m," he said, "this is interesting—very."

"What is?" asked Bailey, joining him.

"This." The window stared directly into the dining room instead of looking outdoors. Bailey stepped back to the corner where the lounge and the dining room joined the central room at ninety degrees.

"But that can't be," he protested, "that window is maybe fifteen, twenty feet from the dining room."

"Not in a tesseract," corrected Teal. "Watch." He opened the window and stepped through, talking back over his shoulder as he did so.

From the point of view of the Baileys he simply disappeared.

But not from his own viewpoint. It took him some seconds to catch his breath. Then he cautiously disentangled himself from the rosebush to which he had become almost irrevocably wedded, making a mental note the while never again to order landscaping which involved plants with thorns, and looked around him.

He was outside the house. The massive bulk of the ground-floor room thrust up beside him. Apparently he had fallen off the roof.

He dashed around the corner of the house, flung open the front door, and hurried up the stairs. "Homer!" he called out, "Mrs. Bailey! I've found a way out!"

Bailey looked annoyed rather than pleased to see him. "What happened to you?"

"I fell out. I've been outside the house. You can do it just as easily—just step through those French windows. Mind the rosebush, though—we may have to build another stairway."

"How did you get back in?"

"Through the front door."

"Then we shall leave the same way. Come, my dear." Bailey set his hat firmly on his head and marched down the stairs, his wife on his arm.

Teal met them in the lounge. "I could have told you that wouldn't work," he announced. "Now here's what we have to do: As I see it, in a four-dimensional figure a three-dimensional man has two choices every time he crosses a line of juncture, like a wall or a threshold. Ordinarily he will make a ninety-degree turn through the fourth dimension, only he doesn't feel it with his three dimensions. Look." He stepped through the very window that he had fallen out of a moment before. Stepped through and arrived in the dining room, where he stood, still talking.

"I watched where I was going and arrived where I intended to." He stepped back into the lounge. "The time before I didn't watch and I moved on through normal space and fell out of the house. It must be a matter of subconscious orientation."

"I'd hate to depend on subconscious orientation when I step out for the morning paper."

"You won't have to; it'll become automatic. Now to get out of the house this time—Mrs. Bailey, if you will stand here with your back to the window, and jump backward, I'm pretty sure you will land in the garden."

Mrs. Bailey's face expressed her opinion of Teal and his ideas. "Homer Bailey," she said shrilly, "are you going to stand there and let him suggest such——"

"But Mrs. Bailey," Teal attempted to explain, "we can tie a rope on you and lower you down eas——"

"Forget it, Teal." Bailey cut him off brusquely. "We'll have to find a better way than that. Neither Mrs. Bailey nor I are fitted for jumping."

Teal was temporarily nonplussed; there ensued a short silence. Bailey broke it with, "Did you hear that, Teal?"

"Hear what?"

"Someone talking off in the distance. D'you s'pose there could be someone else in the house, playing tricks on us, maybe?"

"Oh, not a chance. I've got the only key."

"But I'm sure of it," Mrs. Bailey confirmed. "I've heard them ever since we came in. Voices. Homer, I can't stand much more of this. Do something."

"Now, now, Mrs. Bailey," Teal soothed, "don't get upset. There can't be anyone else in the house, but I'll explore and make sure. Homer, you stay here with Mrs. Bailey and keep an eye on the rooms on this floor." He passed from the lounge into the ground-floor room and from there to the kitchen and on into the bedroom. This led him back to the lounge by a straight-line route; that is to say, by going straight ahead on the entire trip he returned to the place from which he started.

"Nobody around," he reported. "I opened all of the doors and windows as I went—all except this one." He stepped to the window opposite the one through which he had recently fallen and thrust back the drapes.

He saw a man with back toward him, four rooms away. Teal snatched open the French window and dived through it, shouting, "There he goes now! Stop, thief!"

The figure evidently heard him; it fled precipitately. Teal pursued, his gangling limbs stirred to unanimous activity, through drawing room, kitchen, dining room, lounge— room after room, yet in spite of Teal's best efforts he could not seem to cut down the four-room lead that the interloper had started with.

He saw the pursued jump awkwardly but actively over the low sill of a French window and in so doing knock off his hat. When he came up to the point where his quarry had lost his headgear, he stooped and picked it up, glad of an excuse to stop and catch his breath. He was back in the lounge.

"I guess he got away from me," he admitted. "Anyhow, here's his hat. Maybe we can identify him."

Bailey took the hat, looked at it, then snorted and slapped it on Teal's head. It fitted perfectly. Teal looked puzzled, took the hat off, and examined it. On the sweatband were the initials "O.T." It was his own.

Slowly comprehension filtered through Teal's features. He went back to the French window and gazed down the series of rooms through which he had pursued the mysterious stranger. They saw him wave his arms semaphore fashion. "What are you doing?" asked Bailey.

"Come see." The two joined him and followed his stare with their own. Four rooms away they saw the backs of three figures, two male and one female. The taller, thinner of the men was waving his arms in a silly fashion.

Mrs. Bailey screamed and fainted again.

Some minutes later, when Mrs. Bailey had been resuscitated and somewhat composed, Bailey and Teal took stock. "Teal," said Bailey, "I won't waste any time blaming you; recriminations are useless, and I'm sure you didn't plan for this to happen, but I suppose you realize we are in a pretty serious predicament. How are we going to get out of here? It looks now as if we would stay until we starve; every room leads into another room."

"Oh, it's not that bad. I got out once, you know."

"Yes, but you can't repeat it—you tried."

"Anyhow we haven't tried all the rooms. There's still the study."

"Oh, yes, the study. We went through there when we first came in and didn't stop. Is it your idea that we might get out through its windows?"

"Don't get your hopes up. Mathematically, it ought to look into the four side rooms on this floor. Still we never opened the blinds; maybe we ought to look."

" 'Twon't do any harm anyhow. Dear, I think you had best just stay here and rest——"

"Be left alone in this horrible place? I should say not!" Mrs. Bailey was up off the couch where she had been recuperating even as she spoke.

They went upstairs. "This is the inside room, isn't it, Teal?" Bailey inquired as they passed through the master bedroom and climbed up on toward the study. "I mean it was the little cube in your diagram that was in the middle of the big cube, and completely surrounded."

"That's right," agreed Teal. "Well, let's have a look. I figure this window ought to give into the kitchen." He grasped the cords of venetian blinds and pulled them.

It did not. Waves of vertigo shook them. Involuntarily they fell to the floor and grasped helplessly at the pattern on the rug to keep from falling. "Close it! Close it!" moaned Bailey.

Mastering in part a primitive atavistic fear, Teal worked his way back to the window and managed to release the screen. The window had looked *down* instead of *out*, down from a terrifying height.

Mrs. Bailey had fainted again.

Teal went back after more brandy while Bailey chafed her wrists. When she had recovered, Teal went cautiously to the window and raised the screen a crack. Bracing his knees, he studied the scene. He turned to Bailey. "Come look at this, Homer. See if you recognize it."

"You stay away from there, Homer Bailey!"

"Now, Matilda, I'll be careful." Bailey joined him and peered out.

"See up there? That's the Chrysler Building, sure as shooting. And there's the East River, and Brooklyn." They gazed straight down the sheer face of an enormously tall building. More than a thousand feet away a toy city, very much alive, was spread out before them. "As near as I can figure it out, we are looking down the side of the Empire State Building from a point just above its tower."

"What is it? A mirage?"

"I don't think so—it's too perfect. I think space is folded over through the fourth dimension here and we are looking past the fold."

"You mean we aren't really seeing it?"

"No, we're seeing it all right. I don't know what would happen if we climbed out this window, but I for one don't want to try. But what a view! Oh, boy, what a view! Let's try the other windows."

They approached the next window more cautiously, and it was well that they did, for it was even more disconcerting, more reason-shaking, than the one looking down the gasping height of the skyscraper. It was a simple seascape, open ocean and blue sky—but the ocean was where the sky should have been, and contrariwise. This time they were somewhat braced for it, but they both felt seasickness about to overcome them at the sight of waves rolling overhead; they lowered the blind quickly without giving Mrs. Bailey a chance to be disturbed by it.

Teal looked at the third window. "Game to try it, Homer?"

"Hrrumph—well, we won't be satisfied if we don't. Take it easy." Teal lifted the blind a few inches. He saw nothing, and raised it a little more—still nothing. Slowly he raised it until the window was fully exposed. They gazed out at—nothing.

Nothing, nothing at all. What color is nothing? Don't be silly! What shape is it? Shape is an attribute of *something*. It had neither depth nor form. It had not even blackness. It was *nothing*.

Bailey chewed at his cigar. "Teal, what do you make of that?"

Teal's insouciance was shaken for the first time. "I don't know, Homer, I don't rightly know—but I think that window ought to be walled up." He stared at the lowered blind for a moment. "I think maybe we looked at a place where space *isn't*. We looked around a fourth-dimensional corner, and there wasn't anything there." He rubbed his eyes. "I've got a headache."

They waited for a while before tackling the fourth window. Like an unopened letter, it might *not* contain bad news. The doubt left hope. Finally the suspense stretched too thin, and Bailey pulled the cord himself, in the face of his wife's protests.

It was not so bad. A landscape stretched away from them, right side up, and on such a level that the study appeared to be a ground-floor room. But it was distinctly unfriendly.

A hot, hot sun beat down from lemon-colored sky. The flat ground seemed burned a sterile, bleached brown and incapable of supporting life. Life there was, strange stunted trees that lifted knotted, twisted arms to the sky. Little clumps of spiky leaves grew on the outer extremities of these misshapen growths.

"Heavenly day," breathed Bailey, "where is that?"

Teal shook his head, his eyes troubled. "It beats me."

"It doesn't look like anything on earth. It looks more like another planet—Mars, maybe."

"I wouldn't know. But, do you know, Homer, it might be worse than that, worse than another planet, I mean."

"Huh? What's that you say?"

"It might be clear out of our space entirely. I'm not sure that that is our sun at all. It seems too bright."

Mrs. Bailey had somewhat timidly joined them and now gazed out at the outré scene. "Homer," she said in a subdued voice, "those hideous trees—they frighten me."

He patted her hand.

Teal fumbled with the window catch.

"What are you doing?" Bailey demanded.

"I thought if I stuck my head out the window I might be able to look around and tell a bit more."

"Well—all right," Bailey grudged, "but be careful."

"I will." He opened the window a crack and sniffed. "The air is all right, at least." He threw it open wide.

His attention was diverted before he could carry out his plan. An uneasy tremor, like the first intimation of nausea, shivered the entire building for a long second and was gone.

"Earthquake!" They all said it at once. Mrs. Bailey flung her arms around her husband's neck.

Teal gulped and recovered himself, saying, "It's all right,

Mrs. Bailey. This house is perfectly safe. You know you can expect settling tremors after a shock like last night." He had just settled his features into an expression of reassurance when the second shock came. This one was no mild shimmy but the real seasick roll.

In every Californian, native-born or grafted, there is a deep-rooted primitive reflex. An earthquake fills him with soul-shaking claustrophobia which impels him blindly to *get outdoors!* Model Boy Scouts will push aged grandmothers aside to obey it. It is a matter of record that Teal and Bailey landed on top of Mrs. Bailey. Therefore, she must have jumped through the window first. The order of precedence cannot be attributed to chivalry; it must be assumed that she was in readier position to spring.

They pulled themselves together, collected their wits a little, and rubbed sand from their eyes. Their first sensations were relief at feeling the solid sand of the desert land under them. Then Bailey noticed something that brought them to their feet and checked Mrs. Bailey from bursting into the speech that she had ready.

"Where's the house?"

It was gone. There was no sign of it at all. They stood in the center of flat desolation, the landscape they had seen from the window. But aside from the tortured, twisted tree there was nothing to be seen but the yellow sky and the luminary overhead, whose furnacelike glare was already almost insufferable.

Bailey looked slowly around, then turned to the architect. "Well, Teal?" His voice was ominous.

Teal shrugged helplessly. "I wish I knew. I wish I could even be sure that we were on earth."

"Well, we can't stand here. It's sure death if we do. Which direction?"

"Any, I guess. Let's keep a bearing on the sun."

They had trudged on for an undetermined distance

when Mrs. Bailey demanded a rest. They stopped. Teal said in an aside to Bailey, "Any ideas?"

"No . . . no, none. Say, do you hear anything?"

Teal listened. "Maybe—unless it's my imagination."

"Sounds like an automobile. Say, it *is* an automobile!"

They came to the highway in less than another hundred yards. The automobile, when it arrived, proved to be an elderly, puffing light truck, driven by a rancher. He crunched to a stop at their hail. "We're stranded. Can you help us out?"

"Sure. Pile in."

"Where are you headed?"

"Los Angeles."

"Los Angeles? Say, where is this place?"

"Well, you're right in the middle of the Joshua-Tree National Forest."

The return was as dispiriting as the Retreat from Moscow. Mr. and Mrs. Bailey sat up front with the driver while Teal bumped along in the body of the truck and tried to protect his head from the sun. Bailey subsidized the friendly rancher to detour to the tesseract house, not because they wanted to see it again, but in order to pick up their car.

At last the rancher turned the corner that brought them back to where they had started. But the house was no longer there.

There was not even the ground-floor room. It had vanished. The Baileys, interested in spite of themselves, poked around the foundations with Teal.

"Got any answers for this one, Teal?" asked Bailey.

"It must be that on the last shock it simply fell through into another section of space. I can see now that I should have anchored it at the foundations."

"That's not all you should have done."

"Well, I don't see that there is anything to get downhearted about. The house was insured, and we've learned an amazing lot. There are possibilities, man, possibilities! Why, right now I've got a great new revolutionary idea for a house—"

Teal ducked in time. He was always a man of action.

Narrow Valley

R. A. LAFFERTY

Like almost any work by this irrepressible
and inexhaustible Oklahoman, the Lafferty
story that follows is part science fiction, part
tall tale, part sheer magic—a wild and unpre-
dictable extravaganza involving scientists, Indians, and a valley of most remarkable
topological properties.

In the year 1893, land allotments in severalty were made
to the remaining eight hundred and twenty-one Pawnee Indians. Each would receive one hundred and sixty acres of
land and no more, and thereafter the Pawnees would be
expected to pay taxes on their land, the same as the White-
Eyes did.

"Kitkehahke!" Clarence Big-Saddle cussed. "You can't
kick a dog around proper on a hundred and sixty acres.
And I sure am not hear before this pay taxes on land."

Clarence Big-Saddle selected a nice green valley for his
allotment. It was one of the half-dozen plots he had always
regarded as his own. He sodded around the summer lodge
that he had there and made it an all-season home. But he
sure didn't intend to pay taxes on it.

So he burned leaves and bark and made a speech:

"That my valley be always wide and flourish and green
and such stuff as that!" he orated in Pawnee chant style,
"but that it be narrow if an intruder come."

He didn't have any balsam bark to burn. He threw on a

little cedar bark instead. He didn't have any elder leaves. He used a handful of jack-oak leaves. And he forgot the word. How you going to work it if you forget the word?

"Petahauerat!" he howled out with the confidence he hoped would fool the fates.

"That's the same long of a word," he said in a low aside to himself. But he was doubtful. "What am I, a White Man, a burr-tailed jack, a new kind of nut to think it will work?" he asked. "I have to laugh at me. Oh well, we see."

He threw the rest of the bark and the leaves on the fire, and he hollered the wrong word out again.

And he was answered by a dazzling sheet of summer lightning.

"Skidi!" Clarence Big-Saddle swore. "It worked. I didn't think it would."

Clarence Big-Saddle lived on his land for many years, and he paid no taxes. Intruders were unable to come down to his place. The land was sold for taxes three times, but nobody ever came down to claim it. Finally, it was carried as open land on the books. Homesteaders filed on it several times, but none of them fulfilled the qualification of living on the land.

Half a century went by. Clarence Big-Saddle called his son.

"I've had it, boy," he said. "I think I'll just go in the house and die."

"Okay, Dad," the son Clarence Little-Saddle said. "I'm going in to town to shoot a few games of pool with the boys. I'll bury you when I get back this evening."

So the son Clarence Little-Saddle inherited. He also lived on the land for many years without paying taxes.

There was a disturbance in the courthouse one day. The place seemed to be invaded in force, but actually there were but one man, one woman, and five children. "I'm Robert Rampart," said the man, "and we want the Land Office."

"I'm Robert Rampart Junior," said a nine-year-old gangler, "and we want it pretty blamed quick."

"I don't think we have anything like that," the girl at the desk said. "Isn't that something they had a long time ago?"

"Ignorance is no excuse for inefficiency, my dear," said Mary Mabel Rampart, an eight-year-old who could easily pass for eight and a half. "After I make my report, I wonder who will be sitting at your desk tomorrow."

"You people are either in the wrong state or the wrong century," the girl said.

"The Homestead Act still obtains," Robert Rampart insisted. "There is one tract of land carried as open in this county. I want to file on it."

Cecilia Rampart answered the knowing wink of a beefy man at a distant desk. "Hi," she breathed as she slinked over. "I'm Cecilia Rampart, but my stage name is Cecilia San Juan. Do you think that seven is too young to play ingenue roles?"

"Not for you," the man said. "Tell your folks to come over here."

"Do you know where the Land Office is?" Cecilia asked.

"Sure. It's the fourth left-hand drawer of my desk. The smallest office we got in the whole courthouse. We don't use it much anymore."

The Ramparts gathered around. The beefy man started to make out the papers.

"This is the land description," Robert Rampart began. "Why, you've got it down already. How did you know?"

"I've been around here a long time," the man answered.

They did the paper work, and Robert Rampart filed on the land.

"You won't be able to come onto the land itself, though," the man said.

"Why won't I?" Rampart demanded. "Isn't the land description accurate?"

"Oh, I suppose so. But nobody's ever been able to get to the land. It's become a sort of joke."

"Well, I intend to get to the bottom of that joke," Rampart insisted. "I will occupy the land, or I will find out why not."

"I'm not sure about that," the beefy man said. "The last man to file on the land, about a dozen years ago, wasn't able to occupy the land. And he wasn't able to say why he couldn't. It's kind of interesting, the look on their faces after they try it for a day or two and then give it up."

The Ramparts left the courthouse, loaded into their camper, and drove out to find their land. They stopped at the house of a cattle and wheat farmer named Charley Dublin. Dublin met them with a grin which indicated he had been tipped off.

"Come along if you want to, folks," Dublin said. "The easiest way is on foot across my short pasture here. Your land's directly west of mine."

They walked the short distance to the border.

"My name is Tom Rampart, Mr. Dublin." Six-year-old Tom made conversation as they walked. "But my name is really Ramires, and not Tom. I am the issue of an indiscretion of my mother in Mexico several years ago."

"The boy is a kidder, Mr. Dublin," said the mother, Nina Rampart, defending herself. "I have never been in Mexico, but sometimes I have the urge to disappear there forever."

"Ah yes, Mrs. Rampart. And what is the name of the youngest boy here?" Charles Dublin asked.

"Fatty," said Fatty Rampart.

"But surely that is not your given name?"

"Audifax," said five-year-old Fatty.

"Ah well, Audifax, Fatty, are you a kidder, too?"

"He's getting better at it, Mr. Dublin," Mary Mabel said. "He was a twin till last week. His twin was named Skinny. Mama left Skinny unguarded while she was out tippling, and there were wild dogs in the neighborhood. When Mama got back, do you know what was left of Skinny? Two neck bones and an ankle bone. That was all."

"Poor Skinny," Dublin said. "Well, Rampart, this is the fence and the end of my land. Yours is just beyond."

"Is that ditch on my land?" Rampart asked.

"That ditch *is* your land."

"I'll have it filled in. It's a dangerous deep cut even if it is narrow. And the other fence looks like a good one, and I sure have a pretty plot of land beyond it."

"No, Rampart, the land beyond the second fence belongs to Hollister Hyde," Charley Dublin said. "That second fence is the *end* of your land."

"Now, just wait a minute, Dublin! There's something wrong here. My land is one hundred and sixty acres, which would be a half mile on a side. Where's my half-mile width?"

"Between the two fences."

"That's not eight feet."

"Doesn't look like it, does it, Rampart? Tell you what— there's plenty of throwing-sized rocks around. Try to throw one across it."

"I'm not interested in any such boys' games," Rampart exploded. "I want my land."

But the Rampart children *were* interested in such games. They got with it with those throwing rocks. They winged them out over the little gully. The stones acted funny. They hung in the air, as it were, and diminished in size. And they were small as pebbles when they dropped down, down into the gully. None of them could throw a stone across that ditch, and they were throwing kids.

"You and your neighbor have conspired to fence open land for your own use," Rampart charged.

"No such thing, Rampart," Dublin said cheerfully. "My land checks perfectly. So does Hyde's. So does yours, if we knew how to check it. It's like one of those trick topological drawings. It really is a half mile from here to there, but the eye gets lost somewhere. It's your land. Crawl through the fence and figure it out."

Rampart crawled through the fence and drew himself up to jump the gully. Then he hesitated. He got a glimpse of just how deep that gully was. Still, it wasn't five feet across.

There was a heavy fence post on the ground, designed for use as a corner post. Rampart upended it with some effort. Then he shoved it to fall and bridge the gully. But it fell short, and it shouldn't have. An eight-foot post should bridge a five-foot gully.

The post fell into the gully and rolled and rolled and rolled. It spun as though it were rolling outward, but it made no progress except vertically. The post came to rest on a ledge of the gully, so close that Rampart could almost reach out and touch it, but it now appeared no bigger than a match stick.

"There is something wrong with that fence post, or with the world, or with my eyes," Robert Rampart said. "I wish I felt dizzy so I could blame it on that."

"There's a little game that I sometimes play with my neighbor Hyde when we're both out," Dublin said. "I've a heavy rifle and I train it on the middle of his forehead as he stands on the other side of the ditch apparently eight feet away. I fire it off then (I'm a good shot), and I hear it whine across. It'd kill him dead if things were as they seem. But Hyde's in no danger. The shot always bangs into that little scuff of rocks and boulders about thirty feet below him. I can see it kick up the rock dust there, and the sound of it rattling into those little boulders comes back to me in about two and a half seconds."

A bull-bat (poor people call it the night-hawk) raveled around in the air and zoomed out over the narrow ditch, but it did not reach the other side. The bird dropped below ground level and could be seen against the background of the other side of the ditch. It grew smaller and hazier as though at a distance of three or four hundred yards. The white bars on its wings could no longer be discerned; then the bird itself could hardly be discerned; but it was far short of the other side of the five-foot ditch.

A man identified by Charley Dublin as the neighbor Hollister Hyde had appeared on the other side of the little ditch. Hyde grinned and waved. He shouted something but could not be heard.

"Hyde and I both read mouth," Dublin said, "so we can talk across the ditch easy enough. Which kid wants to play chicken? Hyde will barrel a good-sized rock right at your head, and if you duck or flinch, you're chicken."

"Me! Me!" Audifax Rampart challenged. And Hyde, a big man with big hands, did barrel a fearsome jagged rock right at the head of the boy. It would have killed him if things had been as they appeared. But the rock diminished to nothing and disappeared into the ditch. Here was a phenomenon—things seemed real-sized on either side of the ditch, but they diminished coming out over the ditch either way.

"Everybody game for it?" Robert Rampart Junior asked.

"We won't get down there by standing here," Mary Mabel said.

"Nothing wenchered, nothing gained," said Cecilia. "I got that from an ad for a sex comedy."

Then the five Rampart kids ran down into the gully. Ran *down* is right. It was almost as if they ran down the vertical face of a cliff. They couldn't do that. The gully was no wider than the stride of the biggest kids. But the gully diminished those children; it ate them alive. They were doll-sized. They were acorn-sized. They were running for minute after minute across a ditch that was only five feet across. They were going, deeper in it, and getting smaller. Robert Rampart was roaring his alarm, and his wife, Nina, was screaming. Then she stopped. "What am I carrying on so loud about?" she asked herself. "It looks like fun. I'll do it, too."

She plunged into the gully, diminished in size as the children had done, and ran at a pace to carry her a hundred yards away across a gully only five feet wide.

That Robert Rampart stirred things up for a while then. He got the sheriff there, and the highway patrolmen. A ditch had stolen his wife and five children, he said, and maybe had killed them. And if anybody laughs, there may be another killing. He got the colonel of the State National Guard there, and a command post set up. He got a couple or airplane pilots. Robert Rampart had one quality: when he hollered, people came.

He got the newsmen out from T-Town and the eminent scientists, Dr. Velikof Vonk, Arpad Arkabaranan, and Willy McGilly. That bunch turns up every time you get on a good one. They just happen to be in that part of the country where something interesting is going on.

They attacked the thing from all four sides and the top and by inner and outer theory. If a thing measures a half mile on each side and the sides are straight, there just has to be something in the middle of it. They took pictures from the air, and they turned out perfect. They proved that Robert Rampart had the prettiest hundred and sixty acres in the country, the larger part of it being a lush green valley, and all of it being a half mile on a side, and situated just where it should be. They took ground-level photos then, and it showed a beautiful half-mile stretch of land between the boundaries of Charley Dublin and Hollister Hyde. But a man isn't a camera. None of them could see that beautiful spread with the eyes in their heads. Where was it?

Down in the valley itself everything was normal. It really was a half mile wide and no more than eighty feet deep with a very gentle slope. It was warm and sweet and beautiful with grass and grain.

Nina and the kids loved it, and they rushed to see what squatter had built that little house on their land. A house or a shack. It had never known paint, but paint would have spoiled it. It was built of split timbers dressed near smooth with ax and drawknife, chinked with white clay, and sodded up to about half its height. And there was an interloper standing by the little lodge.

"Here, here, what are you doing on our land?" Robert Rampart Junior demanded of the man. "Now you just shamble off again wherever you came from. I'll bet you're a thief too, and those cattle are stolen."

"Only the black-and-white calf," Clarence Little-Saddle said. "I couldn't resist him, but the rest are mine. I guess I'll just stay around and see that you folks get settled all right."

"Is there any wild Indians around here?" Fatty Rampart asked.

"No, not really. I go on a bender about every three months and get a little bit wild, and there's a couple Osage boys from Gray Horse that get noisy sometimes, but that's about all," Clarence Little-Saddle said.

"You certainly don't intend to palm yourself off on us as an Indian," Mary Mabel challenged. "You'll find us a little too knowledgeable for that."

"Little girl, you might as well tell this cow there's no room for her to be a cow since you're so knowledgeable. She thinks she's a shorthorn cow named Sweet Virginia. I think I'm a Pawnee Indian named Clarence. Break it to us real gentle if we're not."

"If you're an Indian where's your war bonnet? There's not a feather on you anywhere."

"How you be sure? There's a story that we got feathers instead of hair on—aw, I can't tell a joke like that to a little girl! How come you're not wearing the Iron Crown of Lombardy if you're a white girl? How you expect me to believe you're a little white girl and your folks came from Europe a couple hundred years ago if you don't wear it? There were six hundred tribes, and only one of them, the Oglala Sioux, had the war bonnet, and only the big leaders,

never more than two or three of them alive at one time,
wore it."

"Your analogy is a little strained," Mary Mabel said.
"Those Indians we saw in Florida and the one at Atlantic
City had war bonnets, and they couldn't very well have
been the kind of Sioux you said. And just last night on the
TV in the motel, those Massachusetts Indians put a war
bonnet on the President and called him the Great White
Father. You mean to tell me that they were all phonies?
Hey, who's laughing at who here?"

"If you're an Indian where's your bow and arrow?" Tom
Rampart interrupted. "I bet you can't even shoot one."

"You're sure right there," Clarence admitted. "I never
shot one of those things but once in my life. They used to
have an archery range in Boulder Park over in T-Town,
and you could rent the things and shoot at targets tied to
hay bales. Hey, I barked my whole forearm and nearly
broke my thumb when the bowstring thwacked home. I
couldn't shoot that thing at all. I don't see how anybody
ever could shoot one of them."

"Okay, kids," Nina Rampart called to her brood. "Let's
start pitching this junk out of the shack so we can move in.
Is there any way we can drive our camper down here,
Clarence?"

"Sure, there's a pretty good dirt road, and it's a lot wider
than it looks from the top. I got a bunch of green bills in an
old night charley in the shack. Let me get them, and then
I'll clear out for a while. The shack hasn't been cleaned out
for seven years, since the last time this happened. I'll show
you the road to the top, and you can bring your car down
it."

"Hey, you old Indian, you lied!" Cecilia Rampart shrilled
from the doorway of the shack. "You *do* have a war bonnet. Can I have it?"

"I didn't mean to lie, I forgot about that thing," Clarence
Little-Saddle said. "My son Clarence Bare-Back sent that

to me from Japan for a joke a long time ago. Sure, you can have it."

All the children were assigned tasks carrying the junk out of the shack and setting fire to it. Nina Rampart and Clarence Little-Saddle ambled up to the rim of the valley by the vehicle road that was wider than it looked from the top. "Nina, you're back! I thought you were gone forever," Robert Rampart jittered at seeing her again. "What—where are the children?"

"Why, I left them down in the valley, Robert. That is, ah, down in that little ditch right there. Now you've got me worried again. I'm going to drive the camper down there and unload it. You'd better go on down and lend a hand too, Robert, and quit talking to all these funny-looking men here."

And Nina went back to Dublin's place for the camper.

"It would be easier for a camel to go through the eye of a needle than for that intrepid woman to drive a car down into that narrow ditch," the eminent scientist Dr. Velikof Vonk said.

"You know how that camel does it?" Clarence Little-Saddle offered, appearing of a sudden from nowhere. "He just closes one of his own eyes and flops back his ears and plunges right through. A camel is mighty narrow when he closes one eye and flops back his ears. Besides, they use a big-eyed needle in the act."

"Where'd this crazy man come from?" Robert Rampart demanded, jumping three feet in the air. "Things are coming out of the ground now. I want my land! I want my children! I want my wife! Whoops, here she comes driving it. Nina, you can't drive a loaded camper into a little ditch like that! You'll be killed or collapsed!"

Nina Rampart drove the loaded camper into the little ditch at a pretty good rate of speed. The best of belief is that she just closed one eye and plunged right through. The car diminished and dropped, and it was smaller than a toy car. But it raised a pretty good cloud of dust as it bumped for several hundred yards across a ditch that was only five feet wide.

"Rampart, it's akin to the phenomenon known as looming, only in reverse," the eminent scientist Arpad Arkabaranan explained as he attempted to throw a rock across the narrow ditch. The rock rose very high in the air, seemed to hang at its apex while it diminished to the size of a grain of sand, and then fell into the ditch not six inches of the way across. There isn't anybody going to throw across a half-mile valley even if it looks five feet. "Look at a rising moon sometime, Rampart. It appears very large, as though covering a great sector of the horizon, but it only covers one half of a degree. It is hard to believe that you could set seven hundred and twenty of such large moons side by side around the horizon, or that it would take one hundred and eighty of the big things to reach from the horizon to a point overhead. It is also hard to believe that your valley is five hundred times as wide as it appears, but it has been surveyed, and it is."

"I want my land. I want my childen. I want my wife," Robert chanted dully. "Damn, I let her get away again."

"I tell you, Rampy," Clarence Little-Saddle squared on him, "a man that lets his wife get away twice doesn't deserve to keep her. I give you till nightfall; then you forfeit. I've taken a liking to the brood. One of us is going to be down there tonight."

After a while a bunch of them were off in that little tavern on the road between Cleveland and Osage. It was only a half mile away. If the valley had run in the other direction, it would have been only six feet away.

"It is a psychic nexus in the form of an elongated dome," said the eminent scientist Dr. Velikof Vonk. "It is maintained subconsciously by the concatenation of at least two minds, the stronger of them belonging to a man dead for many years. It has apparently existed for a little less than a hundred years, and in another hundred years it will be considerably weakened. We know from our checking out of folk tales of Europe as well as Cambodia that these ensorcelled areas seldom survive for more than two hundred and fifty years. The person who first set such a thing in being will usually lose interest in it, and in all worldly things, within a hundred years of his own death. This is a simple thanatopsychic limitation. As a short-term device, the thing has been used several times as a military tactic.

"This psychic nexus, as long as it maintains itself, causes group illusion, but it is really a simple thing. It doesn't fool birds or rabbits or cattle or cameras, only humans. There is nothing meteorological about it. It is strictly psychological. I'm glad I was able to give a scientific explanation to it or it would have worried me."

"It is the continental fault coinciding with a noospheric fault," said the eminent scientist Arpad Arkabaranan. "The valley really is a half mile wide, and at the same time it really is only five feet wide. If we measured correctly, we would get these dual measurements. Of course it is meteorological! Everything including dreams is meteorological. It is the animals and cameras which are fooled, as lacking a true dimension; it is only humans who see the true duality. The phenomenon should be common along the whole continental fault where the earth gains or loses a half mile that has to go somewhere. Likely it extends through the whole sweep of the Cross Timbers. Many of those trees appear twice, and many do not appear at all. A man in the proper state of mind could farm that land or raise cattle on it, but it doesn't really exist. There is a clear parallel in the Luftspiegelungthal sector in the Black Forest of Germany which exists, or does not exist, according to the circumstances and to the attitude of the beholder. Then we have the case of Mad Mountain in Morgan County, Tennessee, which isn't there all the time, and also the Little Lobo Mirage south of Presidio, Texas, from which twenty thousand barrels of water were pumped in one two-and-a-half-year period before the mirage reverted to mirage status. I'm glad I was able to give a scientific explanation to this, or it would have worried me."

"I just don't understand how he worked it," said the eminent scientist Willy McGilly. "Cedar bark, jack-oak leaves, and the word 'Petahauerat.' The thing's impossible! When I was a boy and we wanted to make a hideout, we used bark from the skunk-pruce tree, the leaves of a box elder, and the word was 'Boadicea.' All three elements are wrong here. I cannot find a scientific explanato to this or it would have worried me."

They went back to Narrow Valley. Robert Rampart was still chanting dully: "I want my land. I want my children. I want my wife."

Nina Rampart came chugging up out of the narrow ditch in the camper and emerged through that little gate a few yards down the fence row.

"Supper's ready and we're tired of waiting for you, Robert," she said. "A fine homesteader you are! Afraid to come onto your own land! Come along now; I'm tired of waiting for you."

"I want my land! I want my children! I want my wife!" Robert Rampart still chanted. "Oh, there you are, Nina. You stay here this time. I want my land! I want my children! I want an answer to this terrible thing."

"It is time we decided who wears the pants in this family," Nina said stoutly. She picked up her husband, slung him over her shoulder, carried him to the camper and dumped him in, slammed (as it seemed) a dozen doors at once, and drove furiously down into Narrow Valley, which already seemed wider.

Why, that place was getting normaler and normaler by the minute! Pretty soon it looked almost as wide as it was supposed to be. The psychic nexus in the form of an elongated dome had collapsed. The continental fault that coincided with the noospheric fault had faced facts and decided to conform. The Ramparts were in effective possession of their homestead, and Narrow Valley was as normal as any place anywhere.

"I have lost my land," Clarence Little-Saddle moaned. "It was the land of my father, Clarence Big-Saddle, and I meant it to be the land of my son Clarence Bare-Back. It looked so narrow that people did not notice how wide it was, and people did not try to enter it. Now I have lost it."

Clarence Little-Saddle and the eminent scientist Willy McGilly were standing on the edge of Narrow Valley, which now appeared its true half-mile extent. The moon was just rising, so big that it filled a third of the sky. Who would have imagined that it would take a hundred and eighty of such monstrous things to reach from the horizon to a point overhead, and yet you could sight it with sighters and figure it so.

"I had the little bear-cat by the tail, and I let go," Clarence groaned. "I had a fine valley for free, and I have lost it. I am like that hard-luck guy in the funny paper or Job in the Bible. Destitution is my lot."

Willy McGilly looked around furtively. They were alone on the edge of the half-mile-wide valley."

"Let's give it a booster shot," Willy McGilly said.

Hey, those two got with it! They started a snapping fire and began to throw the stuff onto it. Bark from the dog-elm tree—how do you know it won't work?

It *was* working! Already the other side of the valley seemed a hundred yards closer, and there were alarmed noises coming up from the people in the valley.

Leaves from a black-locust tree—and the valley narrowed still more! There was, moreover, terrified screaming of both children and big people from the depths of Narrow Valley, and the happy voice of Mary Mabel Rampart chanting, "Earthquake! Earthquake!"

"That my valley be always. wide and flourish and such

stuff, and green with money and grass!" Clarence Little-Saddle orated in Pawnee chant style, "but that it be narrow if intruders come, smash them like bugs!"

People, that valley wasn't over a hundred feet wide now, and the screaming of the people in the bottom of the valley had been joined by the hysterical coughing of the camper car starting up.

Willy and Clarence threw everything that was left on the fire. But the word? The word? Who remembers the word?

"Corsicanatexas!" Clarence Little-Saddle howled out with confidence he hoped would fool the fates.

He was answered not only by a dazzling sheet of summer lightning, but also by thunder and raindrops.

"Chahiksi!" Clarence Little-Saddle swore. "It worked. I didn't think it would. It will be all right now. I can use the rain."

The valley was again a ditch only five feet wide.

The camper car struggled out of Narrow Valley through the little gate. It was smashed flat as a sheet of paper, and the screaming kids and people in it had only one dimension.

"It's closing in! It's closing in!" Robert Rampart roared, and he was no thicker than if he had been made out of cardboard.

"We're smashed like bugs," the Rampart boys intoned. "We're thin like paper."

"*Mort, ruine, ecrasement!*" spoke-acted Cecilia Rampart like the great tragedienne she was.

"Help! Help!" Nina Rampart croaked, but she winked at Willy and Clarence as they rolled by. "This homesteading jag always did leave me a little flat."

"Don't throw those paper dolls away. They might be the Ramparts," Mary Mabel called.

The camper car coughed again and bumped along on level ground. This couldn't last forever. The car was widening out as it bumped along.

"Did we overdo it, Clarence?" Willy McGilly asked. "What did one flat-lander say to the other?"

"Dimension of us never got around," Clarence said, "No, I don't think we overdid it, Willy. That car must be eighteen inches wide already, and they all ought to be normal by the time they reach the main road. The next time I do it, I think I'll throw wood-grain plastic on the fire to see who's kidding who."

Wall of Darkness

ARTHUR C. CLARKE

This is an early and relatively little known story by the famed author of *Childhood's End* and *2001: A Space Odyssey*. But it has all the familiar virtues of Arthur C. Clarke's fiction: the rich lyric beauty, the unhurried narrative sweep, and the keen-minded exploration of strange scientific concepts.

Many and strange are the universes that drift like bubbles in the foam upon the river of time. Some—a very few—move against or athwart its current; and fewer still are those that lie forever beyond its reach, knowing nothing of the future or the past. Shervane's tiny cosmos was not one of these: its strangeness was of a different order. It held one world only—the planet of Shervane's race—and a single star, the great sun Trilorne that brought it life and light.

Shervane knew nothing of night, for Trilorne was always high above the horizon, dipping near it only in the long months of winter. Beyond the borders of the Shadow Land, it was true, there came a season when Trilorne disappeared below the edge of the world, and a darkness fell in which nothing could live. But even then the darkness was not absolute, though there were no stars to relieve it.

Alone in its little cosmos, turning the same face always toward its solitary sun, Shervane's world was the last and the strangest jest of the Maker of Stars.

Yet as he looked across his father's lands, the thoughts

46

that filled Shervane's mind were those which any human child might have known. He felt awe, and curiosity, and a little fear, and above all a longing to go out into the great world before him. These things he was still too young to do, but the ancient house was on the highest ground for many miles, and he could look far out over the land that would one day be his.

When he turned to the north, with Trilorne shining full upon his face, he could see many miles away the long line of mountains that curved around to the east, rising higher and higher, until they disappeared behind him in the direction of the Shadow Land.

On his left was the ocean, only a few miles away, and sometimes Shervane could hear the thunder of the waves as they fought and tumbled on the gently sloping sands. No one knew how far the ocean reached. Ships had set out across it, sailing northward while Trilorne rose higher and higher in the sky and the heat of its rays grew ever more intense. Long before the great sun had reached the zenith, they had been forced to return. If the mythical Fire Lands did indeed exist, no man could ever hope to reach their burning shores.

All the inhabited countries of Shervane's world lay in the narrow belt between burning heat and insufferable cold. In every land the far north was an unapproachable region smitten by the fury of Trilorne. And to the south of all countries lay the vast and gloomy Shadow Land, where Trilorne was never more than a pale disk on the horizon and often was not visible at all.

These things Shervane learned in the years of his childhood, and in those years he had no wish to leave the wide lands between the mountains and the sea.

Since the dawn of time his ancestors and the races before them had toiled to make these lands the fairest in the world. There were gardens bright with strange flowers; there were streams that trickled gently between moss-grown rocks to be lost in the pure waters of the tideless sea. There were fields of grain that rustled continually in the wind, as if the generations of seeds yet unborn were talking one to the other. In the great meadows and among the trees the friendly cattle wandered aimlessly with foolish cries. And there was the great house, with its enormous rooms and its endless corridors, vast enough in reality but huger still to the mind of a child.

This was the world in which Shervane had passed his years, the world he knew and loved. As yet, what lay beyond its borders had not concerned his mind.

But Shervane's universe was not one of those free from the domination of Time. The harvest ripened and was gathered into the granaries; Trilorne rocked slowly through its little arc of sky, and with the passing seasons Shervane's mind and body grew. His land seemed smaller now: the mountains were nearer and the sea was only a brief walk from the great house. He began to learn of the world in which he lived, and to be made ready for the part he must play in its shaping.

Some of these things he learned from his father Sherval, but most he was taught by Grayle, who had come across the mountains in the days of his father's father and had now been tutor to three generations of Shervane's family. He was fond of Grayle, though the old man taught him many things he had no wish to learn, and the years of his boyhood passed pleasantly enough until the time came for him to go through the mountains into the lands beyond. Ages ago his family had come from the great countries of the east, and in every generation since, the eldest son had made that pilgrimage again to spend a year of his youth among his cousins. It was a wise custom, for beyond the mountains much of the knowledge of the past still lingered, and there one could meet men from other lands and study their ways.

In the last spring before his son's departure, Sherval collected three of his servants and certain animals it is convenient to call horses and took Shervane to see those parts of the land he had never visited before. They rode west to the sea and followed the coast for many days until Trilorne was noticeably nearer the horizon. Still they went south, their shadows lengthening before them, turning again to the east only when the rays of the sun seemed to have lost all their power. They were now well within the limits of the Shadow Land.

Shervane was riding beside his father, watching the changing landscape with eager curiosity. His father was talking about the soil, describing the crops that could be grown here and those which must fail if the attempt were made. But Shervane's attention was elsewhere: he was staring out across the desolate Shadow Land, wondering how far it stretched and what mysteries it held.

"Father," he said presently, "if you went south in a straight line, right across the Shadow Land, would you reach the other side of the world?"

His father smiled.

"Men have asked that question for centuries," he said, "but there are two reasons why they will never know the answer."

"What are they?"

"The first, of course, is the darkness and the cold. Even here, nothing can live during the winter months. But there is a better reason, though I see that Grayle has not spoken of it."

"I don't think he has; at least, I do not remember."

For a moment Sherval did not reply. He stood up in his stirrups and surveyed the land to the south.

"Once I knew this place well," he said to Shervane. "Come—I have something to show you."

They turned away from the path they had been following and for several hours rode once more with their backs to the sun. The land was rising slowly now, and Shervane saw that they were climbing a great ridge of rock that pointed like a dagger into the heart of the Shadow Land. They came presently to a hill too steep for the horses to ascend, and here they dismounted and left the animals in the servants' charge.

"There is a way around," said Sherval, "but it is quicker for us to climb than to take the horses to the other side."

The hill, though steep, was only a small one, and they reached its summit in a few minutes. At first Shervane could see nothing he had not seen before: there was only the same undulating wilderness, that seemed to become darker and more forbidding with every yard of distance from Trilorne.

He turned to his father with some bewilderment, but Sherval pointed to the far south and drew a careful line along the horizon.

"It is not easy to see," he said quietly. "My father showed it to me from this same spot, many years before you were born."

Shervane stared into the dusk. The southern sky was so dark as to be almost black, and it came down to meet the edge of the world. But not quite, for along the horizon, in a great curve dividing land from sky yet seeming to belong to neither, was a band of deeper darkness, black as the utter night which Shervane had never known.

He looked at it steadfastly for a long time, and perhaps some hint of the future crept into his soul, for the darkling land seemed suddenly alive and waiting. When at last he tore his eyes away, he knew that nothing would ever be the same again, though he was still too young to recognize the challenge for what it was.

And so, for the first time in his life, Shervane saw the Wall.

In the early spring he said farewell to his people, and went with one servant over the mountains into the great lands of the eastern world. Here he met the men who

shared his ancestry, and here he studied the history of his
race, the arts that had grown from ancient times, and the
sciences that ruled the lives of men. In the places of learning he made friends with boys who had come from lands
even farther to the east: few of these he was likely to see
again, but one was to play a greater part in his life than
either could have imagined. Brayldon's father was a famous
architect, but his son intended to eclipse him. He was
traveling from land to land, always learning, watching, ask-
ing questions. Though he was only a few years older than
Shervane, his knowledge of the world was infinitely greater
—or so it seemed to the younger boy.

Between them they took the world to pieces and rebuilt
it according to their desires. Brayldon dreamed of cities
whose great avenues and stately towers would shame even
the wonders of the past; Shervane's interests lay more with
the people who would dwell in those cities and the way
they ordered their lives.

They often spoke of the Wall, which Brayldon knew from
the stories of his own people, though he himself had never
seen it. Far to the south of every country, it lay like a great
barrier athwart the Shadow Land. In high summer it could
be reached, though with difficulty, but nowhere was there
any way of passing it, and none knew what lay beyond. A
hundred times the height of a man, it encircled the entire
world, never pausing even when it reached the wintry sea
that washed the shores of the Shadow Land. Travelers had
stood upon those lonely beaches, scarcely warmed by the
last thin rays of Trilorne, and had seen how the shadowy
Wall marched out to sea contemptuous of the waves
beneath its feet. And on the far shores other travelers had
watched it come striding in across the ocean, to sweep past
them on its journey round the world.

"One of my uncles," said Brayldon, "once reached the
Wall when he was a young man. He did it for a wager, and
he rode for ten days before he came beneath it. I think it

frightened him—it was so huge and cold. He could not tell whether it was made of metal or of stone, and when he shouted, there was no echo at all, but his voice died away quickly as if the Wall swallowed the sound. My people believe it is the end of the world, and there is nothing beyond."

"If that were true," Shervane replied with irrefutable logic, "the ocean would have poured over the edge before the Wall was built."

"Not if Kyrone built it when He made the world, as the legends have it."

Shervane did not agree. "My people believe it is the work of man—perhaps the engineers of the First Dynasty, who made so many wonderful things. If they really had ships that could reach the Fire Lands—and even ships that could fly—they might have possessed enough wisdom to build the Wall."

Brayldon shrugged. "We can never know the answer, so why worry about it?"

This eminently practical advice, as Shervane had discovered, was all that ordinary men ever gave him. Only philosophers were interested in unanswerable questions: To most people, the enigma of the Wall, like the problem of existence itself, was a thing of no practical importance. And all the philosophers he had met had given him different answers.

First there had been Grayle, whom he had questioned on his return from the Shadow Land. The old man had looked at him quietly and said, "There is only one thing behind the Wall, so I have heard. And that is Madness."

Then there had been Artex, who was so old that he could scarcely hear Shervane's nervous questioning. He had gazed at the boy through eyes that seemed too tired to open fully and had replied after a long time: "Kyrone built the Wall in the third day of the making of the world. What is beyond, we shall discover when we die—for there go the souls of all the dead."

Yet Irgan, who lived in the same city, had flatly contradicted this. "Only memory can answer your question, my son. For behind the Wall is the land in which we lived before our births."

Whom could he believe? The truth was that no one knew: if the knowledge had ever existed, it had been lost ages since.

Though this quest was unsuccessful, Shervane had learned many things in his year of study. With the returning spring he said farewell to Brayldon and his other friends and set out along the ancient road that led back to his own country. Once again he made the perilous journey through the great mountain pass, where walls of ice hung threatening against the sky. He came to the place where the road curved down once more toward the world of men, where there was warmth and running water and the breath no longer labored in the freezing air. Here, on the last rise of the road before it descended into the valley, one could see far out across the land to the distant gleam of the ocean. And there, almost lost in the mists at the edge of the world, Shervane could see the line of shadow that was his own country.

He went on down the great ribbon of stone until he came to the bridge that men had built across the cataract in the ancient days. But the bridge was gone: the storms and avalanches of early spring had swept away one of the mighty piers, and the beautiful metal rainbow lay a twisted ruin in the spray and foam a thousand feet below. The summer would have come and gone before the road could be opened once more.

He paused on the last curve of the road, looking back toward the unattainable land that held all the things he loved. But the mists had closed over it, and he saw it no more. Resolutely he turned back along the road until the open lands had vanished and the mountains enfolded him again.

Brayldon was still in the city when Shervane returned.

He was surprised and pleased to see his friend, and together they discussed what should be done in the year ahead. Shervane's cousins, who had grown fond of their guest, were glad to see him again, but their kindly suggestion that he should devote another year to study was not well received.

Shervane's plan had matured slowly, in the face of considerable opposition. Even Brayldon was not enthusiastic at first, and much argument was needed before he would cooperate. But after that, the agreement of everyone else who mattered was only a question of time.

Summer was approaching when the two boys set out toward Brayldon's country. They rode swiftly, for the journey was a long one and must be completed before Trilorne began its winter fall. When they reached the lands that Brayldon knew, they made certain inquiries which caused much shaking of heads. But the answers they obtained were accurate, and soon they were deep in the Shadow Land, and for the second time in his life Shervane saw the Wall.

It seemed not far away when they first came upon it, rising from a bleak and lonely plain. Yet they rode endlessly across that plain before the Wall grew perceptibly nearer—and then they had almost reached its base before they realized how close they were, for there was no way of judging its distance until one could reach out and touch it.

When Shervane gazed up at the monstrous ebony plane that had so troubled his mind, it seemed to be overhanging, about to crush him beneath its falling weight. With difficulty, he tore his eyes away from the hypnotic sight and went nearer to examine the material of which the Wall was built.

It was true, as Brayldon had told him, that it felt cold to the touch—colder than it had any right to be, even in this sun-starved land. It felt neither hard nor soft, for its texture eluded the hand in a way that was difficult to analyze. Shervane had the impression that something was preventing him from actual contact with the surface, yet he could see no space between the Wall and his fingers when he forced them against it. Strangest of all was the uncanny silence of which Brayldon's uncle had spoken: every word was deadened, and all sounds died away with unnatural swiftness.

Brayldon had unloaded some tools and instruments from the packhorses and had begun to examine the Wall's surface. He found very quickly that no drills or cutters would mark it in any way, and presently he came to the conclusion Shervane had already reached. The Wall was not merely adamant; it was unapproachable.

At last, in disgust, he took a perfectly straight metal rule and pressed its edge against the Wall. While Shervane held a mirror to reflect the feeble light of Trilorne along the line of contact, Brayldon peered at the rule from the other side. It was as he had thought: an infinitely narrow streak of light showed unbroken between the two surfaces.

Brayldon looked thoughtfully at his friend.

"Shervane," he said, "I don't believe the Wall is made of matter as we know it."

"Then perhaps the legends are right—those that say it was never built at all, but created as we see it now."

"I think so too," said Brayldon. "The engineers of the First Dynasty had such powers. There are some very ancient buildings in my land that seem to have been made in a single operation from a substance that shows absolutely no sign of weathering. If it were black instead of colored, it would be very much like the material of the Wall."

He put away his useless tools and began to set up a simple portable theodolite.

"If I can do nothing else," he said with a wry smile, "at least I can find exactly how high it is!"

When they looked back for their last view of the Wall, Shervane wondered if he would ever see it again. There was nothing more he could learn. For the future he must forget this foolish dream that he might one day master its secret. Perhaps there was no secret at all—perhaps beyond the Wall the Shadow Land stretched round the curve of the world until it met that same barrier again. That, surely, seemed the likeliest thing. But if it were so, then why had the Wall been built, and by what race?

With an almost angry effort of will he put these thoughts aside and rode forward into the light of Trilorne, thinking of a future in which the Wall would play no more part than it did in the lives of other men.

So two years had passed before Shervane could return to his home. In two years, especially when one is young, much can be forgotten and even the things nearest the heart lose their distinctness so that they can no longer be clearly recalled. When Shervane came through the last foothills of the mountains and was again in the country of his childhood, the joy of his homecoming was mingled with a strange sadness.

The news of his return had gone before him, and soon he saw far ahead a line of horses galloping along the road. He pressed forward eagerly, wondering if Sherval would be there to greet him, and was a little disappointed when he saw that Grayle was leading the procession.

Shervane halted as the old man rode up to his horse. Then Grayle put his hand upon his shoulder, but for a while he turned away his head and could not speak.

And presently Shervane learned that the storms of the year before had destroyed more than the ancient bridge, for lightning had brought his own home in ruins to the ground. Years before the appointed time, all the lands that Sherval had owned had passed into the possession of his son. Far more, indeed, than these, for the whole family had been assembled, according to its yearly custom, in the great house when the fire had come down upon it.

In a single moment of time everything between the mountains and the sea had passed into his keeping. He was the richest man his land had known for generations; and all these things he would have given to look again into the calm gray eyes of the father he would see no more.

Trilorne had risen and fallen in the sky many times since Shervane had taken leave of his childhood on the road before the mountains. The land had flourished in the passing years, and the possessions so suddenly become his had steadily increased their value. He had husbanded them well, and now he had time once more in which to dream. More than that—he had the wealth to make his dreams come true.

Often stories had come across the mountains of the work Brayldon was doing in the east, and although the two friends had never met since their youth they had exchanged messages regularly. Brayldon had achieved his ambitions: not only had he designed the two largest buildings erected since the ancient days, but a whole new city had been planned by him, though it would not be completed in his lifetime.

Hearing of these things, Shervane remembered the aspirations of his own youth, and his mind went back across the years to the day when they had stood together beneath the majesty of the Wall. For a long time he wrestled with his thoughts, fearing to revive old longings that might not be assuaged again. At last he made his decision and wrote to Brayldon—for what was the value of wealth and power unless they could be used to shape one's dreams?

Then Shervane waited, wondering if Brayldon had forgotten the past in the years that had brought him fame. He had not long to wait: Brayldon could not come at once, for he had great works to carry to their completion, but when they were finished, he would join his old friend.

Early the next summer he came, and Shervane met him

on the road below the bridge. They had been boys when they last parted, and now they were nearing middle age, yet as they greeted one another the years seemed to fall away. Each was secretly glad to see how lightly Time had touched the friend he remembered.

They spent many days in conference together, considering the plans that Brayldon had drawn up. The work was an immense one and would take many years to complete, but it was possible to a man of Shervane's wealth. Before he gave his final assent, he took his friend to see Grayle.

The old man had been living for some years in the little house that Shervane had built him. For a long time he had played no active part in the life of the great estates, but his advice was always forthcoming when it was needed, and it was invariably wise.

Grayle knew why Brayldon had come to this land and he expressed no surprise when the architect unrolled his sketches. The largest drawing showed the elevation of the Wall, with a great stairway rising along its side from the plain beneath. At six equally spaced intervals the slowly ascending ramp leveled out into wide platforms, the last of which was only a short distance below the summit of the Wall. Springing from the stairway at a score of places along its length were flying buttresses which to Grayle's eye seemed very frail and slender for the work they had to do. Then he realized that the great ramp would be largely self-supporting, and on one side all the lateral thrust would be taken by the Wall itself.

He looked at the drawing in silence for a while and then remarked quietly, "You always managed to have your way, Shervane. I might have guessed that this would happen in the end."

"Then you think it a good idea?" Shervane asked. He had never acted against the old man's advice and was anxious to have it now.

As usual Grayle came straight to the point. "How much will it cost?"

Brayldon told him, and for a moment there was a shocked silence.

"That includes," the architect said hastily, "the building of a good road across the Shadow Land and the construction of a small town for the workmen. The stairway itself is made from about a million identical blocks which can be dovetailed together to form a rigid structure. We shall make these, I hope, from the minerals we find in the Shadow Land."

He sighed a little.

"I should have liked to have built it from metal rods, jointed together, but that would have cost even more, for all the material would have to be brought over the mountains."

Grayle examined the drawing more closely. "Why have you stopped short of the top?" he asked.

Brayldon looked at Shervane, who answered the question with a trace of embarrassment.

"I want to be the only one to make the final ascent," he replied. "The last stage will be by a lifting machine on the highest platform. There may be danger: that is why I am going alone."

That was not the only reason, but it was a good one. Behind the Wall, so Grayle had once said, lay Madness. If that were true, no one else need face it.

Grayle was speaking once more in his quiet, dreamy voice.

"In that case," he said, "what you do is neither good nor bad, for it concerns you alone. If the Wall was built to keep something from our world, it will still be impassable from the other side."

Brayldon nodded.

"We had thought of that," he said with a touch of pride.

"If the need should come, the ramp can be destroyed in a moment by explosives at selected spots."

"That is good," the old man replied. "When the work is finished, I hope I shall still be here."

Before the winter came, the road to the Wall had been marked out and the foundations of the temporary town laid. Most of the materials Brayldon needed were not hard to find, for the Shadow Land was rich in minerals. He had also surveyed the Wall itself and chosen the spot for the stairway. When Trilorne began to dip below the horizon, Brayldon was well content with the work that had been done.

By the next summer the first of the myriad concrete blocks had been made and tested to Brayldon's satisfaction, and before winter came again some thousands had been produced and part of the foundations laid. Leaving a trusted assistant in charge of the production, Brayldon could now return to his interrupted work. When enough of the blocks had been made, he would be back to supervise the building, but until then his guidance would not be needed.

Two or three times in the course of every year, Shervane rode out to the Wall to watch the stockpiles growing into great pyramids, and four years later Brayldon returned with him. Layer by layer the lines of stone started to creep up the flanks of the Wall, and the slim buttresses began to arch out into space. For a third of every year the work had to be abandoned, and there were anxious months in the long winter when Shervane stood on the borders of the Shadow Land, listening to the storms that thundered past him into the reverberating darkness. But Brayldon had built well, and every spring the work was standing unharmed.

The last stones were laid seven years after the beginning of the work. Standing a mile away so that he could see the structure in its entirety, Shervane remembered with wonder how all this had sprung from the few sketches Brayldon had shown him years ago, and he knew something of the emotion the artist feels when his dreams become reality. And he remembered too the day when, as a boy by his father's side, he had first seen the Wall far off against the dusky sky on the Shadow Land.

There were guardrails around the upper platform. Shervane did not care to go near its edge. The ground was at a dizzying distance, and he tried to forget his height by helping Brayldon and the workmen erect the simple hoist that would lift him the remaining twenty feet. When it was ready, he stepped into the machine and turned to his friend with all the assurance he could muster.

"I shall be gone only a few minutes," he said with elaborate casualness. "Whatever I find, I'll return immediately."

He could hardly have guessed how small a choice was his.

Grayle was now almost blind and would not know another spring. But he recognized the approaching footsteps and greeted Brayldon by name before his visitor had time to speak.

"I am glad you came," he said. "I've been thinking of everything you told me, and I believe I know the truth at last. Perhaps you have guessed it already."

"No," said Brayldon. "I have been afraid to think of it."

The old man smiled a little.

"Why should one be afraid of something, merely because it is strange? The Wall is wonderful, yes—but there's nothing terrible about it, to those who will face its secret without flinching.

"When I was a boy, Brayldon, my old master once said that time could never destroy the truth—it could only hide it among legends. He was right. From all the fables that have gathered around the Wall, I can now select the ones that are part of history.

"Long ago, Brayldon, when the First Dynasty was at its

height, Trilorne was hotter than it is now and the Shadow Land was fertile and inhabited—as perhaps one day the Fire Lands may be when Trilorne is old and feeble. Men could go southward as they pleased, for there was no Wall to bar the way. Many must have done so, looking for new lands in which to settle. What happened to Shervane befell them also, and it must have wrecked many minds—so many that the scientists of the First Dynasty built the Wall to prevent madness from spreading through the land. I cannot believe that this is true, but the legend says that it was made in a single day, with no labor, out of a cloud that encircled the world."

He fell into a reverie, and for a moment Brayldon did not disturb him. His mind was far in the past, picturing his world as a perfect globe floating in space while the Ancient Ones threw that band of darkness around the equator.

False though that picture was in its most important detail, he could never wholly erase it from his mind.

As the last few feet of the Wall moved slowly past his eyes, Shervane needed all his courage to prevent him from crying out to be lowered again. He remembered certain terrible stories he had once dismissed with laughter. But what if, after all, those stories had been true, and the Wall had been built to keep some horror from the world?

He tried to forget these thoughts and found it not hard to do so once he had passed the topmost level of the Wall. At first he could not interpret the picture his eyes brought him; then he saw that he was looking across an unbroken black sheet whose width he could not judge.

The little platform came to a stop, and he noted with half-conscious admiration how accurate Brayldon's calculations had been. Then, with a last word of assurance to the group below, he stepped onto the Wall and began to walk steadily forward.

At first it seemed as if the plain before him was infinite,

for he could not even tell where it met the sky. But he walked on unfaltering, keeping his back upon Trilorne.

There was something wrong: it was growing darker with every step he took. Startled, he turned around and saw that the disk of Trilorne had now become pale and dusky, as if seen through a darkened glass. With mounting fear he realized that this was by no means all that had happened. Trilorne was smaller than the sun he had known all his life.

He shook his head in an angry gesture of defiance. These things were fancies; he was imagining them. Indeed, they were so contrary to all experience that somehow he no longer felt frightened but strode resolutely forward with only a glance at the sun behind.

When Trilorne had dwindled to a point and the darkness was all around him, it was time to abandon pretense. A wiser man would have turned back there and then, and Shervane had a sudden nightmare vision of himself lost in this eternal twilight between earth and sky, unable to retrace the path that led to safety. Then he told himself that as long as he could see Trilorne at all he could be in no real danger.

He went on, with many backward glances at the faint guiding light behind him. Trilorne itself had vanished, but there was still a dim glow in the sky to mark its place. And presently he needed its aid no longer, for far ahead a second light was appearing in the heavens.

At first it seemed only the faintest of glimmers. When he was sure of its existence, he noticed that Trilorne had already disappeared. But he felt more confidence now, and as he moved onward, the returning light helped to subdue his fears.

When he saw that he was indeed approaching another sun, when he could tell beyond any doubt that it was expanding as a moment ago he had seen Trilorne contract, he forced all amazement down into the depths of his mind.

Now at last he could see, faintly through the darkness, the ebon line that marked the Wall's other rim. Soon he would be the first man in thousands of years, perhaps in eternity, to look upon the lands that it had sundered from his world. Would they be as fair as his own, and would there be people there whom he would be glad to greet?

But that they would be waiting, and in such a way, was more than he had dreamed.

Grayle stretched his hand out to the cabinet beside him and fumbled for a large sheet of paper that was lying upon it. Brayldon watched him in silence, and the old man continued.

"How often we have all heard arguments about the size of the universe and whether it has any boundaries! We can imagine no ending to space, yet our minds rebel at the idea of infinity. Some philosophers have imagined that space is limited by curvature in a higher dimension—I expect you know the theory. It may be true of other universes, if they exist, but for ours the answer is more subtle.

"Along the line of the Wall, Brayldon, our universe comes to an end—and yet does not. There was no boundary, nothing to stop one from going onward before the Wall was built. The Wall itself is merely a man-made barrier, sharing the properties of the space in which it lies."

He held the sheet of paper toward Brayldon and slowly rotated it.

"Here," he said, "is a plane sheet. It has, of course, two sides. Can you imagine one that has not?"

Brayldon stared at him in amazement. "That's impossible—ridiculous!"

"But is it?" said Grayle softly. He reached toward the cabinet again and his fingers groped in its recesses. Then he drew out a long, flexible strip of paper.

"We cannot match the intellects of the First Dynasty, but what their minds could grasp directly we can approach by analogy."

He ran his fingers along the paper strip, then joined the two ends together to make a circular loop.

"Here I have a shape which is perfectly familiar to you —the section of a cylinder. I run my finger round the inside, so—and now along the outside. The two surfaces are quite distinct: you can go from one to the other only by moving across the thickness of the strip. Do you agree?"

"Of course," said Brayldon, still puzzled. "But what does it prove?"

"Nothing," said Grayle. "But now watch—"

This sun, Shervane thought, was Trilorne's identical twin. The darkness had now lifted completely, and there was no longer the sensation, which he would not try to understand, of walking across an infinite plain.

He was moving slowly now, for he had no desire to come too suddenly upon that vertiginous precipice. In a little while he could see a distant horizon of low hills, as bare and lifeless as those he had left behind him.

So he walked on; and when presently an icy hand fastened itself upon his heart, he did not pause as a man of lesser courage would have done. Without flinching he watched that shockingly familiar landscape rise around him, until he could see the plain from which his journey had started, and the great stairway itself, and at last Brayldon's anxious, waiting face.

Again Grayle brought the two ends of the strip together, but now he had given it a half twist so that the band was kinked.

"Run your finger around it now," he said quietly.

Brayldon did not need to do so.

"I understand," he said. "You no longer have two separate surfaces. It now forms a single continuous sheet— a one-sided surface—something which at first sight seems impossible."

There was a long, brooding silence. Then Grayle sighed deeply and turned to Brayldon as if he could still see his face.

"Why did you come back before Shervane?" he asked.

"We had to do it," said Brayldon sadly, "but I did not wish to see my work destroyed."

Grayle nodded in sympathy.

"I understand," he said.

Shervane ran his eye up the long flight of steps on which no feet would ever tread again. He felt few regrets: he had striven, and no one could have done more. Such victory as was possible had been his.

Slowly he raised his hand and gave the signal. The Wall swallowed the explosion as it had absorbed all other sounds, but the unhurried grace with which the long tiers of masonry curtsied and fell was something he would remember all his life. For a moment he had a sudden, inexpressibly poignant vision of another stairway, watched by another Shervane, falling in identical chaos on the far side of the Wall.

But that, he realized, was a foolish thought: for none knew better than he that the Wall possessed no other side.

The Destiny of
Milton Gomrath

ALEXEI PANSHIN

In an infinity of possible dimensions there
must surely be worlds better than this one,
right? Right. And if you were magically trans-
ported from this dreary and disappointing
world to the land of your dreams, life would
surely be more romantic and exciting, right?
Well, perhaps not, as Alexei Panshin, the award-
winning author of such novels as *Rite of Passage* and *Star Well*, demonstrates in this
somber little fable.

Milton Gomrath spent his days in dreams of a better life.
More obviously, he spent his days as a garbage collector.
He would empty a barrel of garbage into the back of the
city truck and then lose himself in reverie as the machine
went *clomp, grunch, grunch, grunch*. He hated the truck,
he hated his drab little room, and he hated the endless
serial procession of gray days. His dreams were the sum
of the might-have-beens of his life, and because there was
so much that he was not, his dreams were beautiful.

Milton's favorite dream was one denied those of us who
know who our parents are. Milton had been found in a
strangely fashioned wicker basket on the steps of an or-
phanage, and this left him free as a boy to imagine an infinity of magnificent destinies that could and would be
fulfilled by the appearance of a mother, uncle, or cousin

67

come to claim him and take him to the perpetual June where he of right belonged. He grew up, managed to graduate from high school by the grace of an egalitarian school board that believed everyone should graduate from high school regardless of qualification, and then went to work for the city, all the while holding on to the same well-polished dream.

Then one day he was standing by the garbage truck when a thin, harassed-looking fellow dressed in simple black materialized in front of him. There was no bang, hiss, or pop about it—it was a very businesslike materialization.

"Milton Gomrath?" the man asked, and Milton nodded. "I'm a field agent from Probability Central. May I speak with you?"

Milton nodded again. The man wasn't exactly the mother, or cousin, he had imagined, but the man apparently knew by heart the lines that Milton had mumbled daily as long as he could remember.

"I'm here to rectify an error in the probability fabric," the man said. "As an infant you were inadvertently switched out of your own dimension and into this one. As a result there has been a severe strain on Things-As-They-Are. I can't compel you to accompany me, but, if you will, I've come to restore you to your Proper Place."

"Well, what sort of world is it?" Milton asked. "Is it like this?" He waved at the street and truck.

"Oh, not at all," the man said. "It is a world of magic, dragons, knights, castles, and that sort of thing. But it won't be hard for you to grow accustomed to it. First, it is the place where you rightfully belong, and your mind will be attuned to it. Second, to make things easy for you, I have someone ready to show you your place and explain things to you."

"I'll go," said Milton.

The world grew black before his eyes the instant the words were out of his mouth, and when he could see again, he and the man were standing in the courtyard of a great stone castle. At one side were gray stone buildings; at the other a rose garden with blooms of red and white and yellow. Facing them was a heavily bearded middle-aged man.

"Here we are," said the man in black. "Evan, this is your charge. Milton Gomrath, this is Evan Asperito. He'll explain everything you need to know."

Then the man saluted them both. "Gentlemen, Probability Central thanks you most heartily. You have done a service. You have set things in their Proper Place." And then he disappeared.

Evan, the bearded man, said, "Follow me," and turned. He went inside the nearest building, which appeared to be a barn filled with horses.

He pointed at a pile of straw in one corner. "You can sleep over there."

Then he pointed at a pile of manure, a long-handled fork, and a wheelbarrow. "Put that in that, and take it out and spread it on the rosebushes in the garden. After that, I'll find something else for you to do."

He patted Milton on the back. "I realize it's going to be hard for you at first, boy, but if you have any questions at any time, just ask me."

Stanley Toothbrush

TERRY CARR

Here we have a good-natured, not very serious story which, like some others in this book, involves mysterious disappearances. The disappearers here, though, are neither diplomats nor hospital patients, but words and concepts—banished to a dimension unknown, by the whim of the author and the unexpectedly diabolical talent of his central character.

The trouble was, Herbert decided as he stared baggily into the mirror, that Joanie just didn't understand about mornings. It was very important in this workaday world to understand mornings: each day of the week had a different character, and you had to bear that in mind. Monday, of course, was just awful—it was hopeless morning, when you had five days of work stretching like parallel lines out to eternity or infinity or Friday when they would at last meet. Tuesday was a foggy morning, when the lines were blurred and you didn't want to think about it. By Wednesday you were caught up in the office environment and it seemed somehow, unthinkingly, reasonable that you should spend most of your life doing something you didn't want to do, but Thursday was anxious morning, when it began to dawn on you anew that salvation Friday was coming. And Friday morning was the worst; that was the day when you could no longer resist measuring your sentence in hours.

Today was Friday, and to make it worse Joanie had kept him up till two that morning. A movie, a few drinks afterward at her apartment, and then she'd insisted on just walking around for over an hour, talking. Herbert lathered up his face and painfully began to scratch off the night's accumulation of beard.

He was in a quandary. If he put his foot down and told Joanie right out that he had to get more sleep on week-nights, she'd just get mad and refuse to see him at all, most likely. But if he continued to take her out every night, missing sleep and stumbling around the office the next day like a badly engineered windup toy, it wouldn't be long before he was dismissed. Either way, he'd soon be on the shelf . . . shelved by Joanie or shelved by Mr. Blackburn.

His brain seemed fuzzy, and he found himself thinking irrationally about how silly that expression was. "On the shelf" . . . a ridiculous metaphor. In the first place the word "shelf" was ridiculous all by itself. He ran the word through his brainclouds several times—*shelf, shelf, shelf*. It didn't make sense; it was just a random collection of sounds. Did human animals really go around all the time trying to communicate with such pointless sounds? *Shelf, shelf*.

There was a terrible crashing and banging all through his apartment, and Herbert nearly took off his left nostril with the razor.

He ran out of the bathroom to find out what had happened, heedless of the soapsuds dripping on his living-room rug. The noise had come mostly from the kitchen, and he went there first. He found his dishes (the ones that had been washed and put away) all over the floor in pieces; cans of soup and chili and jars of instant coffee and salad dressing were scattered at his feet. The cupboard doors stood open, one of them still swinging on its hinges.

There was obviously no one else in the apartment, so it must have been an earthquake or something, he decided. He hadn't felt it, but then in his condition this morning that wasn't surprising. He stood staring at the mess and decided that he had a headache too.

Well, there was nothing to do but clear it up. He stooped and began loading cans in his arms, thinking about how much it would cost him to replace the broken dishes, and when he went to put the cans back in the cupboard he found that there were no shelves left.

They weren't anywhere on the floor either; they had disappeared. No shelves? But that was silly. He opened the refrigerator and a head of lettuce rolled out onto the floor and a can of beer fell on his foot. The shelves in the refrigerator had vanished, too.

Herbert didn't like this at all. He put the cans of soup down, kicked some dishes into a corner, and checked the closets. The shelves were gone there too. The bookcase by the door had collapsed, emptying onto the floor two dozen mysteries, short-story collections by Damon Runyon and Ring Lardner, and numerous books on sex in history, secret societies, and the like. When he went back into the bathroom he found that the shelves in the medicine cabinet had gone too, and half his supply of hair tonic was dripping into the sink.

He stood and pondered for a minute. Now let's see . . . he had been shaving and thinking about Joanie, and then he had decided that the word "shelf" was . . . unbelievable. And all the shelves had disappeared, just like that. It was a perfectly clear chain of circumstances.

He decided this was a hell of a way to start a Friday morning.

There wasn't much he could do right now; he was already late at the office. He hurriedly finished shaving, left his razor in the sink, put on a tie, and went to work.

When he entered the office, Marcia frowned at him from behind the switchboard, so he knew Mr. Blackburn was mad. He hung up his coat (noticing that the shelves hadn't disappeared from the closets here) and hurried to his desk.

In a moment the phone rang. "Mr. Blackburn would like you to step into his office," Marcia said.

Herbert went in, carrying with him the list of Los Angeles newspapers he had contacted for the Paperap ads. He didn't suppose he could change the subject, but he might as well try.

"Here's the list you wanted," he said briskly. "I'm not sure about the advisability of this Pasadena thing, but——"

"I wanted that list yesterday," Mr. Blackburn said calmly. "Put it down there. Why were you late this morning?"

"I'm sorry, sir; I had a little trouble at home."

"What kind of trouble?"

All my shelves blinked out of existence, Herbert said in his mind, trying it on for size. No, that wouldn't do at all.

"I cut myself shaving. Couldn't stop the bleeding for almost an hour—must have hit a vein or something. A wonder I didn't bleed to death, sir, ha ha, then I would have been *really* late getting in."

Mr. Blackburn stared coldly at him. "See that it doesn't happen again," he said. "We don't want our employees cutting their throats every morning. Now go away."

Herbert went away. He sat at his desk for ten minutes thinking that he would really have to be sure to come in on time for the next several days. No more nonsense like this morning. And then he sat back in his chair and wondered how one went about seeing that his shelves didn't disappear.

Well, it had happened because he'd decided that "shelf" was a nonsensical word. Presumably it could happen again if he got to thinking about some other words. That newspaper list he'd given to Mr. Blackburn, for instance—what if that had disappeared? After all—*noos-pay-per-list* was pretty silly too. But he'd better not think about that.

His phone rang. "Mr. Blackburn would like you to step into his office," Marcia said.

"Yes, I know," said Herbert, knowing. He went in.

"Where's that list you just gave me?" said Mr. Blackburn.

"I'll look for it again," he said and walked slowly back to his desk. He sorted through various sheets of paper on his desktop and in his drawers and within half an hour was able to make up a duplicate, which he gave to Mr. Blackburn.

Then he sat at his desk and frowned. He didn't like this one bit. He'd read a little about wild talents, of course— people who could tell what cards were before they were turned over, people who could control the roll of dice, who could read minds or see into the future. They were usually erratic, undependable, and often useless—like the lady in Pennsylvania who could tell where every frog within ten miles was at any given time, or the man out in Idaho who could hear the radiation from stars. It was undoubtedly something to do with the unused four fifths of the brain—at least, that was as close as Herbert could come to a rational explanation of it. Something probably caused it.

And now he could make things disappear, snuffed out of existence, just because he didn't believe in certain words. That seemed to him even more unscientific, even more silly —a random wild talent for performing nonsensicalities. He couldn't suppress the feeling that a person with a talent should be able to use it for something useful.

He stared at the blank wall across from him and repeated over and over again in his mind, *Mr. Blackburn, Mr. Blackburn, Mr. Blackburn. . . .*

Then he picked up the phone. "Marcia, is Mr. Blackburn still in his office?"

"Yes; he's on another line," she said.

"Oh." Herbert put the phone back down. Maybe it

wouldn't work with just last names. Knowing a person's True Name had been quite important in magic circles for centuries—if you knew someone's True Name, it had been believed, you had immense power over him.

Perhaps because you could, at will, make him disappear?

He picked up the phone again. "Marcia, what's Mr. Blackburn's full name? His first and middle names, I mean."

"His first name is Chester. Wait a minute, I have his middle name here somewhere. . . ." There was a rustling. "Yes, his middle name is Hartwick, H-a-r-t-w-i-c-k."

"Thank you," Herbert said and hung up. Now that was all very fine—Chester Hartwick Blackburn would be an easy name not to believe in. In fact, Herbert wondered for a moment how Mr. Blackburn had got this far through life without having been snuffed out that way. But perhaps no one else had Herbert's talent.

Chester Hartwick Blackburn, Chester Hartwick Blackburn, Chester Hartwick Blackburn, said Herbert in his mind. What a silly combination of syllables. Of course they were thoroughly meaningless.

He picked up the phone. "Is Mr. Blackburn still on that other line, Marcia?"

"Yes, he is."

"Are you sure? Can you just plug in for a second and see if he's still talking?"

"Just a minute. . . ." There were a few clicks. "Yes, he's still talking. Do you want me to connect you with him when he's off again?"

"God, no," Herbert muttered and hung up.

Well, all right then—he couldn't will people out of existence simply by disbelieving in their names. All that business about True Names had been about some mythical abstraction, anyway, not just the name someone's parents might give them. Who could know what Mr. Blackburn's True Name was?

He stared at the clutter of papers on his desk, focusing

about two inches beyond them and seeing them only as a white blur, while he continued to toy with the whole idea. A lot of the formulas devised by medieval magicians for conjuring the devil and various demons had involved using their True Names. And those strange chants they used in their preparations could have simply been the names of various things, maybe forces, which prevented the other-world beings from getting in—sort of like deciding that doors didn't exist instead of getting up to open one when there was a knock. Maybe those old magicians had sat there muttering "Abracadabra" over and over because an abracadabra was some sort of closed door between this world and another, and if they disbelieved in the word the door would cease to bar the way.

Herbert sat up at his desk and frowned. But of course all this speculation was not only silly, but useless as well. Just the sort of thing a person could get to thinking about on a Friday morning. He hunched over his desk and got busy at his day's work.

That evening when he got home, he carefully cleared up the kitchen and the medicine cabinet and closets and book-cases, stacking cans and bottles and galoshes on the floor or on ledges. ("Ledges" was a good, sensible word, Herbert decided, and carefully refrained from thinking about it anymore.) Then he called Joanie.

"I was thinking of going dancing tonight," he said. "Shall I pick you up around eight?"

There was a short silence on her end. "Oh, Herbie honey, I think you'd better rest tonight—you were up awfully late last night, and you know how you complain. I've invited someone over to watch TV."

Herbert frowned. "But it's Friday night—I don't have to go to work tomorrow."

"Well, just the same, I think you should get some sleep," she said. "You've been looking so tired."

"Joanie, what's come over you?"

She laughed, a soft laugh that he always found delightful. "Well, actually, I've got a new beau, Herbie, and he's taking me out tonight. His name is Stanley."

"Stanley what?" Herbert said in a low voice.

She giggled. "Oh, Herbie! Stanley Toothbrush, then, because he always carries a toothbrush with him in case he ever wants to go somewhere suddenly. He used to live in Chicago, but one time he went to the store to buy some Kleenex and decided to come to New York instead, and he did. He's like that, so I call him Stanley Toothbrush. It fits him so much better than his real name."

"Yes, it seems to," Herbert growled. "Well, I hope the two of you will be very happy."

"What?" she said. "Herbie? You didn't believe me, did you? I was only joking, honey, you know that."

"Were you," he said.

"Well, *of course.* Oh, Herbie, don't be silly. Edna is coming over tonight, and we're going to watch television and do our nails. Honestly!"

"But I wanted to go dancing," he said.

"Well, not tonight, because Edna's on her way here already. Anyway, you ought to be proud of me, because you've been saying for a long time that you need more rest nights, and now I've finally——"

"I guess so," he said, and they said good-bye.

He set about fixing dinner for himself, heating beans and franks. He turned on the burner and slammed the pan down on it and then stood with his hands on his hips, irritably waiting for the water to boil. He usually wasn't so impatient about cooking, but tonight he was in a bad mood. Not enough sleep recently, for one thing.

But Joanie's imaginary boyfriend was worrying him, too. Maybe he wasn't so imaginary at that. And come to think of it, who was Edna? Joanie had never mentioned her before. This was all very suspicious.

Of course, he really needn't worry too much, he thought as he dropped the cold franks into the water. This Stanley Toothbrush didn't sound like much competition—a fellow with so little stability that he'd take off and move a thousand miles to another city overnight couldn't have much to offer a girl. No security, no future. . . . He probably didn't shave, either.

But still, his bipartisan mind told him, Stanley Toothbrush might be a fascinating person . . . just the sort of wild, funloving, carefree Casanova that a girl could ruin herself over. And since he was so lax about responsibilities, he probably didn't have a regular job and was therefore free to take Joanie out every night. He could probably sweep her off her feet while Herbert was struggling to keep his job.

It was all very unfair. Herbert certainly hoped that Stanley Toothbrush really didn't exist, as Joanie had assured him. And in fact, maybe it would be a good idea to do something about that himself. If ever he'd heard a person's True Name, it was Stanley Toothbrush.

Stanley Toothbrush must go. It was a quite senseless name in the first place, easy to disbelieve. *Stanley Toothbrush, Stanley Toothbrush, Stanley Toothbrush.* . . .

At the end of an hour Herbert had to stop repeating Stanley's name in his head. He had said it so often that it had almost begun to sound real.

The next afternoon Herbert went to Joanie's apartment in person. He rang the bell, and the little peephole opened, and he saw Joanie's blue left eye, trimmed with long dark lashes, looking at him.

"It's me," he said.

"Oh! Herbie!" Joanie sounded upset. "Herbie, you'll have to go away. . . . I mean, come back later. I'm not decent."

"At three o'clock in the afternoon?"

"Well, I was going to . . . take a shower. I'm completely *nude*, without a *stitch*."

"That's fine," he said.

"Herbert!"

"All right; I'll come back in half an hour." He went out and killed time looking at the magazines in a drugstore. He saw an ad for some toothpaste, and that reminded him of Stanley Toothbrush, whom he didn't want to think about because he didn't exist anyway, if he had ever existed. If he had, Herbert had done away with him, he hoped.

When he went back to Joanie's apartment and rang, she opened the peephole at him again. "Oh, Herbie, can you——"

"Let me in, Joanie," he said decisively.

"But I'm still not——"

"Your eye is quite thoroughly made up," he said, "and I know that you never do your eyes until you're dressed. Now open the door."

Joanie made a small sound, and her left eyebrow came down to show part of what must have been a much bigger frown. "Well, all right."

She opened the door and Herbert walked in. Standing by the door to the kitchen was a young man who could have been no one but Stanley Toothbrush.

"I didn't want you to—I was trying to get rid of him," Joanie whispered quickly to him and then said aloud, "Herbert, this is Stanley . . . Stanley Toothbrush; I don't know his real last name."

"How do you do," said Herbert evenly.

Stanley Toothbrush waved casually at him, leaning against the wall and displaying even white teeth in a full, friendly smile. He had dark sandy hair and rugged features, and he stood at least six feet tall, much more impressive than Herbert's own five feet nine. His face had a day's stubble.

"We were just going off for a boat ride around Manhattan," said Stanley. "You can come, too; we wouldn't mind."

"No!" said Joanie, and then when Herbert turned to look at her she said, "I mean yes of course you can come, but I was trying to——"

"Fine! Let's all go!" said Stanley, and picked up his weathered brown jacket from where it had been lying over the back of a chair.

Joanie was standing in the middle of the room, looking from one to the other of them helplessly. "I wasn't going to go in the first place," she said.

"But it's all settled," Stanley said reasonably and led the two of them out the door. Herbert followed seethingly, not saying a word.

They caught a cab and arrived at the dock where the excursion boat was tied up just in time for the next trip. Several times Joanie tried to say something to Herbert, but he sat in such stony silence and Stanley continued to chatter so unconcernedly that each time she gave up with a shrug and a little frustrated sound.

"Now don't do anything unnecessary like paying," said Stanley when they approached the ramp. "Leave it to me; I have connections."

"I thought you would," Herbert muttered.

Stanley walked up to the ticket-taker and slapped him on the shoulder. Herbert couldn't hear what he was saying, but Stanley was smiling and laughing and occasionally nodding over at him and Joanie. The ticket man grinned back at him and waved them all on.

As they took their seats by the boat's railing Stanley leaned over and said confidentially to Herbert, "Took a little finagling, but don't worry about it. Had to tell him that Joanie was with you and I was showing the two of you the sights. I gave him a lot of stuff about young lovebirds —it probably would've made you sick to hear it, but he liked it." Then Stanley turned back to Joanie, who had been maneuvered into sitting on his other side, and started telling her about how he had worked for a few days on the building of the very boat they were on.

Herbert didn't listen. He stared blackly into the water which lapped against the boatside, repeating in his head, *Stanley Toothbrush, Stanley Toothbrush*. The name was frighteningly believable.

He looked up when a woman in her fifties sat down next to him, fussing with her bag and struggling to get out of her heavy coat. Herbert helped her with that, and she laid the coat across her ample lap, and then he began to stare into the water again. But she wouldn't let him.

She tapped him on the shoulder. "Do you see the terribly handsome man standing on the quay?" she said softly. "The one with the dog? Well, that's my husband."

"Who, the dog?" said Herbert, coming up out of the water. "Oh, no, I'm sorry. Yes, he's very handsome."

"We were just married last week," she said, "and we've come to the big city for our honeymoon. But he has to stay and wait for me because O'Shaughnessy has heart trouble. He's almost twenty years old."

"Good heavens!" said Herbert, staring at her husband.

"He's an Irish Wolfhound, and he won't drink his water," she said.

"Oh, yes, of course," Herbert said, and just then the boat started backing out from the pier.

He turned back to Stanley and Joanie. Stanley was pointin up the Hudson saying, "There's a fine little park up there, looks out on the river, and is all terraced in the center and wild around the edges. Squirrels and all. We ought to go up there tomorrow."

"Well, I don't—" said Joanie helplessly.

"It's just a quick ride on the subway," Stanley said. "You've still got all those tokens you bought last night, haven't you?"

"Well, yes."

"Then fine, and it won't cost a thing," said Stanley.

"I think I have to powder my nose," she said and got up and went off to the concessions area of the boat. She looked at Herbert as she passed and made a pleading face. Herbert got up and followed her.

She stopped just inside the door to the concessions room. "Herbie honey, I've been trying to get a word in edgeways. Honestly, he just showed up last night, and I'd never seen him before. I can't get rid of him."

"You had a date with me last night," Herbert said. "You could have told him that."

"But I *didn't*. I mean, I'd already told you I was going to stay home, and then Edna said she couldn't come——"

"Well, why was he hanging around anyway, if you didn't encourage him? And what do you mean, he came after you'd told me you were staying home? You'd already made a date with him when I called."

"But I *hadn't*, that's what I'm trying to tell you! I'd never seen him before, and I just made him up to tease you, Herbie. And then there he was, at my door, and what could I do?"

Herbert stared at her. "You really made him up when you were talking to me?"

"Yes, honestly, Herbie."

"And then he showed up, and his name is Stanley Toothbrush?"

"Yes, and he has a toothbrush in his right pants pocket." She waved her hands. "I couldn't get rid of him all night— he insisted and he insisted, and I didn't want to hurt him. He's very sensitive, Herbie, you'd be surprised."

"*All night?*" said Herbert.

"Well, he slept right outside my apartment, right there in the hall, and I couldn't just send him away."

Herbert shook his head. "This has ceased to be ridiculous," he muttered.

"What?"

"Joanie, this is crazy, but you remember what I told you

about the powers of the mind? That book I was reading? Well, *I've got it now!*"

Two passengers who had been standing next to him edged away.

"I mean I've got some crazy kind of wild talent," Herbert said more softly. "Listen, yesterday morning I was shaving, and I started thinking, I don't know why, about what a ridiculous word 'shelf' is. You know, if you say a word over and over often enough it loses all its meaning. So I did that with 'shelf,' and all of a sudden all the shelves in my apartment disappeared!"

"Herbert!"

"No, Joanie, I'm serious. I can show you the apartment— they're all gone, and things are all over the floor. So anyway, last night when you told me about Stanley, I tried to make him disappear, too—but I said his name over and over so much that it began to make *sense*. And that must have been what happened, that's where he came from."

Joanie frowned and pursed her lips. "Herbie, if you're joking——"

"Now, why would I joke about Stanley Toothbrush?" Herbert said. "He's no laughing matter!"

"Then show me," she said.

"What? Show you?"

"Make something disappear." she tapped her foot.

"Well . . . I mean, it's a wild talent, and it may not work just like turning it on and off."

"Herbert."

"All right, I'll try." He looked around the concession area and spotted a man with a red moustache and a derby. He looked ridiculous, but Herbert couldn't decide whether it was the fault of the hat or the moustache. Well, either one would do.

"What do you think of that man over there?" he said to Joanie, and in his mind he said *moustache, moustache*.

"That man?" she said.

"Yes." *Mus-tash*, he thought. *Muss-tash*.

"Oh!" Joanie put her fingers to her mouth in surprise.

The man muttered to his wife, "Demmed dreft in here." She stared at him and shuddered, and pointed, and he wrinkled his mouth and frowned and gasped and ran to the men's room.

Herbert smiled. "You see? And that's where Stanley Toothbrush came from."

"But what are we going to do?" she said.

"I don't know." Herbert's grin vanished. "Every time I try to make him disappear he just gets more real."

"Well, we've got to do something," Joanie said.

Stanley Toothbrush walked up behind them just then and said heartily, "How about something to eat? They have hotdogs here, and hamburgers, anything you want."

"I'm not hungry," Herbert said shortly and went back to his seat by the rail. Stanley steered Joanie to the concessions stand, and she bought two hotdogs.

The woman whose Irish wolfhound had heart trouble said to Herbert, "Have you noticed how wonderfully wet the river is today? The water just goes down and down, fathom after fathom or whatever they are."

"I'm afraid so," Herbert said abstractedly. "I hope your dog gets well soon."

"Oh, he won't," the woman said lightly. "He'll die in a week or so—married life is so hard on him. I'm afraid Arnold and I shock him with our behavior."

"Well, it's terrible when a dog's nerves start acting up," said Herbert, and then he grimaced and wondered why he let himself be drawn into such conversations. He leaned over the rail and stared into the water again.

"It's very wet, very wet," said the woman, "and I suppose there are fish in it."

"It's conceivable," said Herbert, and had a vision of a huge beast of a shark arcing out of the water and snapping Stanley Toothbrush from the boat, glom just like that.

"Oh, dear!" said the woman suddenly, and Herbert looked up to see her pointing frantically down at the river. "I dropped my bag! Oh, my heavens! It's in the water! Back there!"

"Back where?" said Herbert. "It's probably sunk already."

He heard running footsteps, and suddenly Stanley was beside them, taking off his shoes. "You lost your purse, lady?"

"Yes, it's back there!"

"Hold my hotdog," Stanley said and thrust it into the woman's hand and dived overboard. It wasn't a very good dive; he went end over end and hit the water feet first, but he came up sputtering and swam strongly back to the area where the purse had been dropped. A crowd was gathering around Herbert and the woman.

"It's probably sunk to the bottom," Herbert said.

"Well, it was one of those new materials, plastic or something," said the woman, beaming happily at all the attention. "I think it was watertight. It may float."

"Did Stanley go in the water?" Joanie asked, coming up behind them.

"Yes—he's a good swimmer," Herbert said. "I always knew he would be."

The boat blew a whistle and swung around to pick up Stanley, while the loudspeaker told everyone to remain calm and stay in their seats. Stanley had almost reached the purse.

"How gallant of him!" said Joanie. "Herbie, you must admit that was a sweet thing for him to do."

Herbert looked slightly disgusted and shrugged. "It's a Stanley Toothbrush thing to do," he said. "If you're so impressed with him, just remember that I made him up."

"Well, you needn't be short with me," Joanie said. "And anyway, I'll bet Stanley is just some sort of wish fulfillment of yours—he acts the way you secretly wish you could."

She wrinkled her nose at him. "There, you see I read a book or two every now and then myself."

"I don't want to talk about it," said Herbert.

By the time the boat had returned to where Stanley was, he had come up with the purse dripping in his hand. The ship's crew lowered a ladder over the side and gave him a hand up, and Stanley immediately squished in wet stocking feet over to the Irish-wolfhound woman and delivered her purse with a sloshy bow. Then he took his hot dog back from her.

"It was just wonderful of you to swim after it," the woman said to him. "You went over the side like a real-life Sir Walter Raleigh!"

Stanley gave a crooked grin and shrugged. "It wasn't much of a dive," he said around the hot dog.

"Wasn't he wonderful, my dear?" said the woman to Joanie.

"Yes, I thought it was very gallant, that's the only word I can think of," she said.

"If only Arnold could have seen you!" said the woman.

"Arnold is her husband," Herbert explained and added under his breath, "Fortunately, he doesn't have heart trouble, like some dogs I know."

The woman was still beaming delightedly at Stanley, holding her dripping purse. Joanie was fluttering around him, trying to get his shirt off so it would dry, and Herbert felt quite disgusted. He shook his head and walked off around to the other side of the boat.

The rest of the excursion was thoroughly ruined for him. He sat apart from Stanley and Joanie, and when at one point she came over to him, he was irritable and they had words. By the time the boat docked back at its point of departure over an hour later, he was in a vile mood.

Stanley's clothes had dried a bit by then, and he had squeezed back into his shoes. "Well, what shall we do now?" he said lightly as they stepped off the boat.

"I think we should go to Herbert's apartment," said

Joanie. "You could hang your clothes over the radiator, and we could all have a few drinks."

"While he sits there without any clothes on?" cried Herbert.

"Oh, don't be silly; you can lend him some dry clothes to wear," she said and took his arm to lead him off toward a waiting cab.

They did go to Herbert's apartment, and when they came in the door, Herbert remembered that he had meant to buy some new shelves today. Books and cans were still tumbled on the floor, and it looked pretty bad.

Stanley looked around the place and said lightly, "Well, bachelor's apartment, eh? You should get a woman to take care of you, Herbie." Herbert glared at him.

Joanie glanced around briefly and then went to the kitchen, where Herbert always kept a bottle on the drainboard. "I'll mix some drinks," she said, "while you go in the bedroom and get out of those clothes, Stanley."

Stanley grinned and followed Herbert while he found some clean underwear, pants, and shirt for him. He picked the oldest and most faded clothes he had. "Hang the clothes in the shower," he said and went into the kitchen.

Joanie was cross. "You needn't be a bad sport about it," she said. "He does have some good qualities, as you can see."

"His ribs stick out." Herbert said.

"Oh, honestly, Herbie! Your whole attitude toward him is incredible. First you try to tell me that you . . . made him up, or *created* him or something, then you——"

"But I did!" said Herbert. "Or at least you did, and then I brought him into existence by accident. He doesn't even belong here."

"Well, if you brought him into existence or whatever, then it's your own fault and it serves you right," she said. "Anyway, I don't believe that story about you and your whatever-it-is."

"It's a wild talent," said Herbert. "I told you."

"Well, you and your wild talons can just—"

"Wild talent, wild talent!" he said.

"What?"

"*Wild talent!* Good God, can't you——"

"Wild talent, wild talent," she said. "That's a silly name for it, don't you think? Herbie, why don't you go in the bedroom and see if Stanley is still there?"

"Of course he's still there, unless he suddenly went to Chicago," said Herbert.

"I doubt it," Joannie said, grinning. "For one thing, your shelves are back." She waved a hand at the cupboard.

"Well, I'll be damned," Herbert said.

"Not necessarily. But do go see if Stanley is gone, please."

Herbert went. The bedroom was empty, the clothes he had given Stanley were lying on the floor, and though the shower stall showed where his wet clothes had dripped, Stanley Toothbrush wasn't there either.

Herbert went into the kitchen and kissed the back of Joanie's neck. "You're a genius," he said.

"Yes, and what's more I only mixed two drinks," she said. "Now tell me what we're going to do tonight."

Monday morning Herbert stared blearily into the mirror and decided that "morning" was the most ridiculous and idiotic word he had ever heard. But of course it did him no good.

Inside

CAROL CARR

Here is a strange and haunting story, an eerie voyage to other dimensions of the soul. Mysterious, baffling, it offers special rewards for the careful and thoughtful reader. Carol Carr, the wife of editor and writer Terry Carr, shows herself in this piece to be a fascinating and extraordinary author in her own right.

The house was a jigsaw puzzle of many dreams. It could not exist in reality, and, dimly, the girl knew this. But she wandered its changing halls and corridors each day with a mild, floating interest. In the six months she had lived here the house had grown rapidly, spinning out attics, basements, and strangely geometric alcoves with translucent white curtains that never moved. Since she believed she had been reborn in this house, she never questioned her presence in it.

Her bedroom came first. When she woke to find herself in it she was not frightened, and she was only vaguely apprehensive when she discovered that the door opened to blackness. She was not curious, and she was not hungry. She spent most of the first day in her four-poster bed looking at the heavy, flowered material that framed the bay window. Outside the window was a yellow-gray mist. She was not disturbed; the mist was a comfort. Although she experienced no joy, she knew that she loved this room and the small bathroom that was an extension of it.

On the second day she opened the carved doors of the

89

mahogany wardrobe and removed a quilted dressing gown. It was a little large and the sleeves partially covered her hands. Her fingers, long and pale, reached out uncertainly from the edge of the material. She didn't want to open the bedroom door again but felt that she should; if there were something outside to discover, it too would belong to her.

She turned the doorknob and stepped out into a narrow hall paneled, like the wardrobe in her room, in carved mahogany. There were no pictures and no carpet. The polished wood of the floor felt cool against her bare feet. When she had walked the full distance to the end and touched a wall, she turned and walked to the other end. The hall was very long and there were no new rooms leading from it.

When she got back to her bedroom, she noticed a large desk in the corner near the window. She didn't remember a desk but she accepted it as she accepted the rest. She looked out and saw that the mist was still there. She felt protected.

Later that afternoon she began to be hungry. She opened various drawers of the desk and found them empty except for a dusty tin of chocolates. She ate slowly and filled a glass with water from the bathroom sink and drank it all at once. Her mouth tasted bad; she wished she had a toothbrush.

On the second day she had wandered as far as the house allowed her to. Then she slept, woke in a drowsy, numb state, and slept again.

On the third day she found stairs, three flights. They led her down to a kitchen, breakfast area, and pantry. Unlike her room, the kitchen was tiled and modern. She ate a Swiss-cheese sandwich and drank a glass of milk. The trip back to her room tired her and she fell asleep at once.

The house continued to grow. Bedrooms appeared, some like her own, some modern, some a confusion of periods and styles. A toothbrush and a small tube of toothpaste appeared in her medicine cabinet. In each of the bedrooms she found new clothes and wore them in the order of their discovery.

She began to awaken in the morning with a feeling of anticipation. Would she find a chandeliered dining room or perhaps an enclosed porch whose windows looked out on the mist?

At the end of a month the house contained eighteen bedrooms, three parlors, a library, dining room, ballroom, music room, sewing room, a basement, and two attics.

Then the people came. One night she awoke to their laughter somewhere beyond her window. She was furious at the invasion but comforted herself with the thought that they were outside. She would bolt the downstairs door, and even if the mist disappeared, she would not look. But she couldn't help hearing them talk and laugh. She strained to catch the words and hated herself for trying. This was *her* house. She stuffed cotton into her ears and felt shut out rather than shut in, which angered her even more.

The house stopped growing. The mist cleared, and the sun came out. She looked through her window and saw a lake made up of many narrow branches, its surfaces covered with a phosphorescent sparkle like a skin of dirty green sequins. She saw no one—the intruders came late at night, dozens of them, judging from the sound they made.

She lost weight. She looked in the mirror and found her hair dull, her cheeks drawn. She began to wander the house at odd hours. Her dreams were haunted by the voices outside, the splash of water, and, worst of all, the endless laughter. What would these strangers do if she suddenly appeared at the doorway in her quilted robe and demanded that they leave? If she said nothing but hammered a "No Trespass" sign to the oak tree? What if they just stood there, staring at her, laughing?

She continued to wander. There were no new rooms,

but she discovered hidden alcoves and passageways that connected bedroom to bedroom, library to kitchen. She used these passageways over and over again, avoiding the main halls.

Now when she woke, it was with a feeling of dread. Had any of them got in during the night, in spite of her precautions? She found carpenters' tools in a closet and nailed the windows shut. It took weeks to finish the job, and then she realized she had forgotten the windows in the basement. That part of the house frightened her, and she put off going down. But when the voices at night began to sound more and more distinct, when she imagined that they were voices she recognized, she knew that she had no choice.

The basement was dark and damp. She could find no objects to account for the shadows on the walls. There was not enough light to work by, and when she finished, she knew she had done badly. If they really wanted to come in, these crooked nails would not stop them.

The next morning she found that the house had a new wing of three bedrooms. They were smaller than those in the rest of the house, and more cheaply furnished.

She never knew exactly when the servants moved in. She saw the first one, the cook, when she walked into the kitchen one morning. The woman, middle-aged and heavy, wearing a black uniform with white apron, was taking eggs from the refrigerator.

"How would you like them, madam?"

Before she could reply, the doorbell rang. A butler appeared.

"No, don't answer it!" He continued to walk. "Please ____"

"I beg your pardon, madam. I am partially deaf. Would you repeat your statement?"

She screamed: *"Do not answer the door."*

"Scrambled, fried, poached?" said the cook.

"It may be the postman," said the butler.

"Would madam like to see today's menu? Does madam plan to have guests this evening?" The housekeeper was dark and wiry. She hardly moved her lips but her words were clear.

"Some nice cinnamon toast, I think," the cook said, and she placed two slices of bread in the toaster.

"If you're having twelve to dinner, madam, I would suggest the lace cloth," said the housekeeper.

The doorbell was still ringing. It wouldn't stop. She ran to the stairs, toward the safety of her room.

"Madam?" said the cook, the housekeeper, the butler.

That night they came at sunset. She climbed into bed and drew the covers up around her, but still she could hear their laughter, rising and falling. The water made splashing sounds. She pulled the covers over her head and burrowed beneath them.

A new sound reached her and she threw off the covers, straining to hear. They were downstairs, in the dining room. She could make out the clink of silverware against dishes, the kind of laughter and talking that came up at her from the water. The house was alive with a chattering and clattering she could not endure. She would confront them, explain that this was her house; they would have to leave. Then the servants.

She went down the stairs slowly, rehearsing the exact words she would use. When she reached the ballroom floor, she stopped for a second, then crossed it to the open doors of the dining room. She flattened herself against the wall and looked inside.

There were twelve of them, as the housekeeper had suggested—and she knew every one.

Her husband, bald, bold, and precise: "I told her, 'Go ahead and jump; you're not scaring me.' And she jumped. The only brave thing she ever did."

Her mother, dry as a twig, with dead eyes: "I told her it was a sin—but she never listened to me, never."

A friend: "She didn't seem to feel anything. When other

people laughed, she always looked serious, as if she was mulling it over to find the joke."

"She used to laugh when she was very small. Then she stopped."

"She was a bore."

"She was a sparrow."

"She was a failure. Everyone knew. When she found out for herself, she jumped."

"Was it from a bridge? I was always curious about that."

"Yes. They found her floating on the surface, staring into the sun like some would-be Ophelia." Her husband smiled and wiped his lips with a napkin. "I don't think I'll recommend this place. I've got a stomachache."

The others agreed. They all had stomachaches.

The guests returned, night after night, but each night it was a different group. Always she knew them and always she watched as they ate. When the last party left, joking about the food being poisoned, she was alone. She didn't have to dismiss the servants; they were gone the next day. The yellow-gray mist surrounded her windows again, and for the first time she could remember, she laughed.

The Captured
Cross-Section

MILES J. BREUER, M.D.

Dr. Miles J. Breuer, a Nebraska physician, was one of the early favorites of American science-fiction magazine readers. Whenever he could steal time from his medical duties, he relaxed by writing s-f, and in a literary career that lasted from 1927 to 1940 he produced such diverting tales as the classic semantic farce "The Gostak and the Doshes" and the impressive utopian novel *Paradise and Iron*. Fourth-dimensional matters seem to have been a particular preoccupation of his, for he returned to the theme repeatedly, in such stories as "The Appendix and the Spectacles," "The Book of Worlds," and the story reprinted here.

The head of Jiles Heagey, Instructor in Mathematics, was bent low over the sheets of figures; and becomingly close to it leaned the curly-haired one of his fiancée, Sheila Mathers, daughter of the head of the Mathematics Department. Shelia was no mean mathematician herself and had published some original papers.

"Are you trying to tell me that this stuff makes any sense?" she laughed, shaking her head over the stack of papers.

"Your father couldn't follow it either," Heagey answered. "He used abusive language at me when I showed it to him."

"Now don't be mean to my father. Someday you'll learn

that under his blustering exterior he has a heart of gold. But what do these things mean, and what did you bring me in here for?"

"You have followed through Einstein's equation for the transformation of coordinates, have you not?" Heagey explained. "Well, this is Einstein's stuff, only I've carried it farther than he did."

"It doesn't look the same—" Sheila shook her head.

"That is because I am using four coordinates. The most complicated existing equations, with the three coordinates x, y, and z, and involving three equations each with the variables:

$$x_1, \qquad y_1, \qquad z_1,$$
$$x_2, \qquad y_2, \qquad z_2,$$
$$x_3, \qquad y_3, \qquad z_3,$$

require that you keep in mind nine equations at a time. That is a heavy burden, and relatively few men are able to do it. Here I have four coordinates, w, x, y, and z, and the variables:

$$w_1, \qquad x_1, \qquad y_1, \qquad z_1,$$
$$w_2, \qquad x_2, \qquad y_2, \qquad z_2,$$
$$w_3, \qquad x_3, \qquad y_3, \qquad x_3,$$
$$w_4, \qquad x_4, \qquad y_4, \qquad z_4,$$

requiring that I carry in my mind sixteen equations at one time. That may seem impossible, but I've drilled myself at it for two years, and gradually I was able to go farther and farther——"

"But there are other quantities here," Sheila interrupted, studying the paper intently, "that do not belong in equations for the rotation of coordinates. They look like the integrals in electromagnetic equations."

"Good for you!" Heagey cried enthusiastically. "That

pretty little head has something on the inside, too. That is just exactly what they are: electromagnetic integrals. You see, the rotation of coordinates looks very pretty in theory, but when you hook it up with a little practical dynamics—don't you understand yet?"

Sheila stared at the young mathematician in questioning wonder.

"Sheila, jewel, you're just irresistible that way. I can't help it." He gathered her in his arms and kissed her face in a dozen places. She pushed him away.

"No more until you tell me what this is about. I mean it!" She stamped her foot, but a merry smile contradicted her stern frown.

"You're just like your father when you're like that," he said, taking up the papers again. "Very simple little conception," he continued. "Why be satisfied with rotating coordinates on paper? Here's a way to rotate them in concrete, physical reality.

"Listen now. When you rotate two coordinates through ninety degrees, you have an ordinate where there previously was an abscissa. If you rotate three coordinates through ninety degrees, you can make a vertical plane occupy a horizontal position. Now—suppose you rotate four coordinates through forty-five degrees: you can then make a portion of space occupy a new position, outside of what we know as space. And we can bring into this space of ours a portion of the unknown space along the fourth coordinate——"

"The fourth dimension!" gasped Sheila.

"There it is on paper. But we're going to do it in reality. There"—pointing across the room—"are the coils by means of which we can rotate some real space. I want you to see the preliminary trial. As I do not know just exactly what may happen, I am going to rotate only a small portion to begin with."

Sheila's eyes gleamed with excited comprehension.

"Call Father in. He's just across the corridor——"

"Not for the very first trial. I want you to see that alone. After we know what it will do——"

"But it may be dangerous. Something may happen!"

"You think it might injure the furniture or damage the building? For the preliminary trial I shall rotate it only for an instant and turn it back instantly."

She clung to his arm nervously while he grasped the black handle of the switch and threw it down, waited a few seconds, and pulled it out again.

They saw nothing. There was a crash, instantaneously loud, and fading almost instantly to a distant, muffled rumble, and ceasing suddenly. There was a heavy thud and a pounding on the floor. Sheila gave a little scream.

There in front of them was a rapidly moving object; it bounced up and down off the floor to a height of three feet about once a second. It did not have the harmonic motion of a bouncing body, however; it stopped abruptly up in the air and shot downward at high speed, hit the floor, stopped a moment, and shot back upward. Then it stopped suddenly and hung in the air. It was about the size of a large watermelon and looked for all the world like human skin: smooth, uniform, unbroken all around.

The two stared at it amazed. Heagey walked up and touched it with the tip of a finger. It grew smaller. And suddenly it decreased to about one-half its former size, retaining its surface smoothness and uniformity unchanged.

It had felt soft and warm, like human flesh.

Now it was increasing in size again, while they stared gasping, speechless, at it. When it stopped growing suddenly, it was the size of a big barrel, with rounded ends. There was a bulging ridge around the middle, on each side of which was a dark brown strap of something like leather. The rest of it was just naked skin.

Sheila and Heagey stood rooted to the spot, staring at it and at each other. What was the thing? Where had it come from?

The thing began thumping up and down off the floor again, with great, thudding shocks. After a while it desisted and lay still. It was a most uncouth, hideous-looking thing: a great lump of naked flesh with two straps around it. It looked exactly like some huge tumor in a medical museum, or like some monstrosity of birth. Could it be alive?

Both of them approached it cautiously. Heagey pricked it with a pin. The skin was tough and he jabbed hard. A drop of blood appeared.

Then there was a terrible commotion. The object decreased in size to a small sphere like a baseball. In fact, there were several baseball-sized lumps of flesh all around; just naked flesh. They moved rapidly, and two of them were between him and Sheila. Two or three were on the far side of her. He counted ten of them altogether. Five of them closed swiftly around her. Then she was gone!

Her scream, cut suddenly short, still rang in his ears. And she was gone! Suddenly vanished from in front of him! He groped about, feeling for her in the empty air, but there was nothing anywhere. There lay the watermelonlike lump of flesh that he had first seen. It was on the floor and lay quite still. And she was gone! He held his head distractedly.

The door opened and Professor Mathers, Sheila's father, came in.

"What's going on here?" he demanded, blinking his eyes.

Heagey stared blankly, trying to think.

"This thumping and screaming?" the professor continued.

"I think I begin to understand," Heagey began.

"Think you understand!" the professor shouted. "What have you done to my daughter? She doesn't scream for nothing."

He caught sight of the ovoid lump of flesh. He turned pale and stopped as if frozen. Some terrible thought crossed his mind, connecting it with his daughter; had some nefarious experiment turned her into that thing?

"What's that?" he snapped savagely.

"Something's got to be done," Heagey said, chiefly to himself. "We've got to bring her back here. I'm afraid to manipulate the thing too many times; the Lord only knows what else it may dip up."

The professor glared.

"You sound like a first-rate manic-depressive crazy man——"

"Wait till I shut that thing up," Heagey said, getting a hold of himself, "and I'll explain all I know about this. I was getting ready to try to rotate a dog out of space, and so I have a new, strong dog cage here."

He set the dog cage down beside the lump of flesh; very gently, very slowly, he pushed it in. His touch recoiled at the warm, soft feel of it; but he got it into the cage and locked the door. Then he set out a chair for the professor, but his hand shook, for his mind was on Sheila.

He sat down facing the professor, his back to the cage. Suddenly the professor's face fell, and his eyes stared ahead with a look of utter blankness. Heagey whirled around and looked at his "specimen." It was out of the cage!

There hadn't been a sound. His eyes had not been off it for ten seconds. The cage was still locked. There it lay, three feet away from the cage, only it wasn't the same. There were two pieces of it now, long, cylindrical, rounded at the ends. Like a couple of legs without knees or feet. Heagey got up and unlocked the cage, noting that it required fifteen seconds. He felt around inside the cage with his hands but found nothing.

"After all," he sighed, "it is very simple."

The professor stared at him, now thoroughly convinced that he was crazy. Heagey explained about his sixteen equations and how readily they interlocked with the electromagnetic integrals, and of how the very simple application of any form of electromagnetic energy would rotate four coordinates.

"I wanted her to see the preliminary experiment. I used

but little power on a small field. Just opened a little trap door into space, so to speak. There is only one explanation for what has happened here. I rotated a portion of a fourth dimension and left a hole in hyperspace for an instant. Just as if you rotate up a portion of this floor, there will be a hole left. As chance would have it, just at that moment some inhabitant of hyperspace came along and stumbled into it, and I swung back on him and caught him.

"Here he is, stuck. What we see and feel is a cross-section of him, a solid cross-section of that part of him that is cut by our three-dimensional space. See! If I stick my finger through this sheet of paper, the two-dimensional inhabitants on its surface will perceive only a circle. At first the nail occupies a portion of its circumference; as I push my finger on through, the nail is gone, and folds and ridges appear and disappear. If my whole hand goes through, the circle increases greatly in size. If they draw a circle around my finger and try to imprison it, I can withdraw it and stick it through somewhere else, and they cannot understand how it was done——"

"But what about Sheila? Where is she?"

Heagey's face dropped. He had been full of interest and exultation in his problem. The reminder of her was an icy shock.

"There is only one possible conclusion," he went on in a dead voice. "The struggles of the fourth-dimensional creature swept her out into hyperspace."

The professor sprang up and walked rapidly out of the room. There was something determined in his stride. He slammed the door. Heagey sat down and thought. Somehow he must rescue Sheila.

How could it be done? Should he try the rotation again? He had all the figures and could repeat it accurately. But that would not be at all certain to get her back. The captured fourth-dimensional creature might get away. Heagey didn't want to lose him. Not only that he wanted to study him, but somehow he felt that he must hang on to the only link with that world where Sheila was now lost.

The thought of its getting away worried him. How could he make sure that it would not escape? He reasoned back to the plane section of a three-dimensional object. Enclosing it in a circle would do no good. But if tied tightly with a circle of rope, it might be kept from moving up and down. Analogically, if he could get this thing into some sort of a tight bag, he might feel free to flip his trap door once more. Ah! then came the brilliant idea!

He could sally out into hyperspace and look for Sheila!

He got the lump of flesh fastened up tight in a canvas sack and lashed the other end of the stout rope with which he tied it around a concrete pillar. Then the door opened, and two policemen walked in, followed by the professor. He was urging them on. "There he is! Grab him!" he seemed to say in attitude and gesture, though not in words.

A pang of alarm shot through Heagey. He was needed right here to rescue Sheila. What would become of her if they locked him up? His mind, as usual, worked quickly and logically, in contradistinction to the professor's, who seemed to have been thrown into an unreasoning rage by his daughter's disappearance. He sprang to his switchboard and shouted: "Stop!"

Something in his determined attitude alarmed the policemen; his hand on the ominous-looking apparatus might mean something. They stopped.

"What's this? What do you want?" Heagey demanded.

The professor's torrents broke loose.

"He murdered my daughter. Made away with her. I've got a warrant for his arrest. Nonsensical twaddle about the fourth dimension. Prosecute him to the limit: that's what I'll do. Been hanging around her too much. He's crazy. Throw him in jail. Make him bring her back!"

Heagey laughed a desperate laugh, which made the other three more certain that he was a dangerous maniac.

"Like throwing debtors into jail." Heagey derided acidly. "Fat chance of paying the debt then! Move another step, and I'll throw the three of you into unknown hyperspace."

They were all afraid, of they knew not what. Heagey outlined to them that he wanted to go out into hyperspace and search for Sheila. But he would tie himself on a rope fastened at this end. And he wanted someone here at this end, who was friendly to him, to manage things. He telephoned out for a rope and for two of his students. The policemen watched, too puzzled to know what to do. The professor acquiesced, more from fear, like a man at the point of a gun, than because he saw the reason of it.

The rope was delivered and the two students, Adkins and Beemer, arrived. They helped him fix a firm sling around his shoulders, waist, and thighs. The loose rope was coiled up on the floor, several hundred feet of it, and the other end tied to a concrete pillar. There was some amazed staring by the students at the writhing thing in the canvas sack.

"I'll tell you about that later," Heagey said. "All the pointers and dials are set. All you need to do is to throw this switch and jerk it back at once. Adkins, you do that; and, Beemer, you watch the rope. When I signal by jerking it six times, Adkins, you throw the switch again the same way."

That was all. Without another word Adkins threw the switch. There was the same crash, instantaneously muffled and almost suddenly fading away as at a distance. There was a momentary sensation of agitation, though nothing really moved.

Heagey was gone. The loose end of the rope that had tied him lay on the floor. It was certainly a breathless thing. The professor stared with a sort of vacant expression on his face, as though the solid ground had suddenly dropped from beneath his feet. It dawned upon him that perhaps Sheila had really disappeared that way.

Beemer picked up the end of the rope. It was not an end; it merely looked that way. There was a strong tension on it; in fact it soon began to slip through his hands, and coil after coil was drawn off the pile on the floor and simply vanished. For a while it stopped and then went on unwinding.

The policemen gazed blankly. They were unable to understand what had happened. The man they were to arrest had suddenly melted from sight. They mumbled astonished monosyllables to each other. But they were not as astonished as was Professor Mathers. They did not grasp the enormity of what was going on, as he did. It upset his whole mental universe. He sat awhile and then paced nervously up and down the vast room. He came and looked at the rope. Then he looked at the canvas sack. The sack lay loose as though the contents had escaped. He felt of it and found that it contained three soft baseball-sized objects. He jumped back and shrank away from it. The time seemed interminable. He waited and waited.

Besides an occasional mumble between the policemen or a short exclamation from Adkins or Beemer, there was no conversation. Beemer watched the rope closely. There was a tense nervous strain created largely by the professor's distracted movements. Then, after what seemed hours, though in reality less than one hour, there were six short tugs on the rope. Adkins threw his switch, and out of the crash and tremor Heagey tumbled out on the floor, all tangled up in coils of rope.

He was breathless, haggard, wild-eyed. He lay for a moment on the floor, panting. Then he sprang up and gazed fiercely, wildly about. He seemed suddenly to perceive where he was. An expression of relief came over his face; he sighed deeply and sank down to a sitting position. He looked exhausted; his clothes were disarranged and ripped in some places, and were covered with dust.

The five people looked at him in silent amazement. He

looked from one to the other of them; it was a long time before he spoke.

"Good to be back here. I can hardly believe I'm really back. Never again for me."

"What about Sheila? Where is she?" the professor demanded.

Heagey recoiled as though from some shock. He sank again into profound depression. At first he had seemed a little happy to get back. Apparently Sheila had been forcibly driven out of his mind for the time.

"Let me tell you about it," he began slowly. He seemed not to know just how to proceed. "That is, if I can. I don't even know how to tell it. I know what it must feel like to go insane.

"I heard the switch go down as I gave Adkins the signal. Then it seemed like an elevator starting, and that was all. Until I looked around.

"I was sitting on something that looked like rock or cement. Not far from me was that barrellike lump of flesh with the two straps around it, just exactly as I had seen it in the laboratory. And then a row of shapes reaching into the dim, blue distance. The nearer ones seemed to be of concrete or cement. You've heard me jeer at the crazy cubistic and futuristic designs on book wrappers and wallpaper. Well, those are pleasant and harmonious compared with the dizzy, jagged angles, the irregular, zigzag shapes with peaks and slants, and everything out of sense and reason except perspective. Perspective was still correct. Just a long, straight row fading into the distance. What in the world it could be, I hadn't the faintest idea. However, I gradually reasoned it out.

"Naturally, since I am a three-dimensional organism, I can only perceive three dimensions. Even out in hyperspace I can only see three dimensions. What I saw must therefore be the spatial cross-section of some sort of buildings. I couldn't see the entire buildings but merely the cross-section cut by the particular set of coordinates in which I was. Now it occurs to me, that since that barrel-like thing looked exactly the same to me out there as it did in the room here, I must have been in a 'space' or set of coordinates parallel to the ones we are in now.

"Imagine a two-dimensional being, whose life had been confined to a sheet of paper and who could only perceive in two dimensions, suddenly turned loose in a room. He could only see one plane at a time. Everything he saw would be cross-sections of things as we know them. Wouldn't he go crazy? I nearly did.

"I first started out to walk along beside the row of rock-like shapes. Suddenly near me there appeared two spheres of flesh, just like this one we have here. They rapidly increased in size, coalesced into a barrel-shaped thing with a metal-web belt around the middle, and then dwindled quickly; there were three or four smaller gobs of stuff and then ten or a dozen little ones; finally an irregular, blotchy, melonlike thing which quickly disappeared. In fifteen seconds it had all materialized and gone.

"I was beginning to understand the stuff now. Merely some inhabitant or creature of hyperspace going by. As he passed through my particular spatial plane, I saw successive cross-sections of him. Just as though my body were passing through a plane, say feet first: first there would be two irregular circles; then a larger oval, the trunk, with two circles, the arms, at the sides and separate from it; and so on until the top of the head vanished as a small spot.

"I followed down the line of buildings, looking around. Bizarre shapes appeared around me, changing size and shape in the wildest, dizziest, most uncouth ways, splitting into a dozen pieces and coming together into large, irregular chunks. Some seemed to be metal or concrete, some human flesh, naked or clothed. In a few minutes my mind became accustomed to interpreting this passage of fourth-dimensional things through my 'plane,' and I studied them with interest. Then I slipped and fell down. Down I whizzed for a while, and everything about me disappeared.

"I found myself rolling; and sitting up, I looked around again. There was nothing. I still seemed to be on cement or stone, and in all directions it stretched away endlessly into the distance. It was the most disconcerting thing I had ever seen in my life. I was just a speck in a universe of cement pavement. I began to get panicky but controlled myself and started to walk, feeling the reassuring pull of the rope behind me. I walked nervously and saw nothing anywhere. Evidently I had slipped off my former 'plane' and gotten into a new one. The rope tightened suddenly; perhaps I had reached the end of it. It jerked me backward and I swung dizzily, my feet hanging loose.

"I swung among millions of small spherical bodies disposed irregularly in all directions about me, even below. They moved gently back and forth in small arcs; and there were large brown bodies—

"Why go through it all? I stumbled from one spatial plane into another. Each seemed a totally different universe. I couldn't get them correlated in my mind into any kind of a consistent whole at all. For a long time I climbed over some huge metal framework; I ran into moving things that grew larger and disappeared; I struggled through a jungle of some soft, green, vegetable stuff. Just all of a sudden I made up my mind that I'd never find Sheila.

"She might be within a foot of me all the time, yet I couldn't get to her, because I couldn't see out of three dimensions. I yelled her name until I was hoarse and my head throbbed, but nothing happened. I grew panicky and decided I wanted to go back. I pulled on the rope and dragged myself toward the direction from which it came; sometimes I slid rapidly toward it; at others I could feel myself dragging my entire weight with my arms. Then I could go no farther, pull as I might. It seemed like trying to reach an inch higher than you really can; I couldn't quite stretch that far. So I gave it six short tugs. Very quietly I tumbled out here. I haven't seen Sheila."

The professor was calm. His face was set hard.

"Either you're telling the truth or you're insane as a loon," he said, and his voice was puzzled and sincere. "Perhaps I'm crazy, too. I'm broad-minded enough to admit that is possible. I've got you charged with murder. But I'll give you a chance. What are you going to do about Sheila?"

Heagey's eyes blazed.

"You can go to hell with your chance," he roared. "I want Sheila back worse than you do. If anyone can get her back, it is myself. If you interfere, you simply guarantee that she's lost, that's all. If you want to see her again, keep your hands off! See?"

The professor was a better man than his blustering actions might lead one to think.

"Well, I'm worried," he said shortly. "Can I help you any?"

Heagey never changed expression.

"Perhaps you can. I may need more money than I've got. Just now you can help me most by getting out of here and taking everybody with you and letting me think. I've got an idea. I'll phone you when I want something."

"Well, remember you're charged with murder, and there will be a police guard around this place."

How great and yet how small men will be under trying conditions!

Heagey, left alone, sat and thought. He jumped up and ran his hands through his hair.

"God! Think of it!" he gasped. "Sheila out there alone! In that mad place! Not even a rope!"

He paced rapidly around the room. Then he seized paper and pencil and began to draw. He drew circles and ellipsoids of different sizes and laid the drawings in a row. The professor came in an hour later and found him at it.

"How do you ever expect to find her that way?" he growled peevishly.

"Shut up!" Heagey snapped, his nerves tautened into disrespect. He swept up the papers with his hand and crumpled them into the wastebasket. "No use. Can't study four-dimensional stuff on a two-dimensional plane. Say!" he shouted roughly at the professor, "get me a hundred pounds of modeling clay up here. Quick as you can!"

The professor trotted out out after it without a word, much less with any understanding of what it was about.

"Do you think you'll do it?" was his eager attitude one moment, and "If you don't, you go on trial for murder," he raved a moment later.

Far into the night Heagey worked with modeling clay, molding the forms that had appeared in the laboratory and some of those he had seen in hyperspace. He tried to recollect the order in which the various shapes had appeared to him and laid them in rows in that order. Late into the night he modeled and arranged and stared and studied. Near midnight the professor poked his head in the door.

"She's really gone," he moaned. "She hasn't come home. She's nowhere!" He turned on the haggard Heagey. "The policemen are on the job, so don't try to get away. But I'm offering five thousand dollars to anyone who brings Sheila back."

Heagey snatched a few hours' sleep on the floor. In the morning when the professor opened the door, he was arranging clay balls and clubs into rows and staring at them. As soon as the professor's head appeared, he shouted:

"I've got it! The biggest photographs you can get of Sheila. Head and full-length both. And fast! Hurry!"

He now turned his attention to the object in the canvas sack. He untied the rope from the fourteen-ounce duck, tied the corners of the canvas together, inserted a stout stick (obtained by breaking the leg off a chair), and twisted it, squeezing the small ball of flesh unmercifully. At first

sight it was a cruel-looking procedure, but there was method in it. The Thing began to jump back and forth ex-
citedly. He loosened the bulk of his pressure but kept up a
steady, firm tension. His strength was sufficient to hold it
fairly steady. Suddenly he loosened all pressure. The mass
of flesh suddenly grew larger, and the satisfied expression
in Heagey's face showed that was what he was working for.
Just as when you push hard against someone and then
suddenly let go: he falls toward you.

He persisted steadily along this line. When the cross-
section increased in size he held it loosely, patted it gently,
and even talked soothingly. As soon as it started to de-
crease, he screwed up his stick and bore down on it re-
morselessly. For an hour he wrestled. Then the professor
entered with two sixteen-by-twenty photographs taken out
of frames.

"Wait!" shouted Heagey peremptorily. "Stand there and
hold 'em." He twisted up his stick again, held it, and
loosened it; and was rewarded by seeing the barrel-shaped
mass appear; then two long, cylindrical bodies beside it,
covered with metal mesh.

"What's your idea?" the professor asked.

"Don't bother me!" Heagey panted irritatedly. "And
don't move. I might need you any minute."

Finally the Thing decreased in size again; but this time
Heagey seemed satisfied with it. He removed the canvas
sack. There was an irregular sphere the size of a bucket.
Over its surface were queer patches, glassy places, and
iridescent, rainbow spots that changed color and looked
deep.

"Quick now, the pictures!"

Heagey set up the pictures in front of the Thing, as if to
show them to it. The professor stared at him as he would
at a silly child. Heagey suddenly hit himself in the side of
the head with his fist.

"What a prize fool! I keep on being a fool!" he shouted. He turned savagely to the professor.

"Get me the two best fellows out of the Fine Arts Department. Quick! Sculptors!"

If the professor thought Heagey was crazy, nevertheless some glimmer of hope of rescuing Sheila lent him willingness and speed of thinking. He scolded rapidly into the telephone for a few minutes, repeating the word "emergency" several times. Then he started down the driveway, taking a policeman with him.

Heagey was feverishly busy. He seemed to be bringing every object in the room that could be conveniently carried, to set before the unearthly specimen he had there. He seemed to be showing it things. He acted like some ignorant, superstitious savage, bringing things to his god. Books, chairs, hats and coats, mathematical medals, hammers and wrenches, one thing after another; he held them up in front of it for a while and tossed them aside on the growing heap. When the two sculptors arrived, he barked his directions at them and continued what seemed his silly efforts to entertain the object in front of him by showing it everything he could find. At least it remained quiet and unchanged.

The sculptors, infected with his determination, worked rapidly. First there was a model of a heavy, bulging man, with his foot caught in a hole like a coal chute and held fast by a square lid. Then from the pictures a model of Sheila; considering the speed with which it was made, it was a wonderful thing, with her pointed chin and curly hair all true to life. Then a rough model of Heagey.

Heagey set the models down in front of the iridescent, patchy Thing and played puppets with the models, went through a regular dramatic performance with them. The models of Sheila and himself stood near the man caught in the trap door. The imprisoned man struggled and knocked Sheila over, and she rolled away; she fell down off the surface of the block to a lower level. The imprisoned man continued to struggle, and the model of Heagey searched around but could not get past the edge of the block.

Then, very impressively motioning toward the Thing, as though he really believed it was looking, Heagey made the model of the imprisoned man lean over and pick up Sheila and hand her over to the model of himself. The model of himself held on to Sheila and raised the trap door that imprisoned the bulging man, who hopped out of the hole and hastened away. That was the little show that Heagey put on with the yard-high clay models.

The patchy sphere changed suddenly. First it shrank, and then it swelled; then there were three or four Things moving back and forth. And suddenly, there stood Sheila!

Pale and distracted and wan she looked; and she swayed as she looked blankly around. Then her eyes widened, and she gave a little scream; but a look of peace and content spread over her features. By the time Heagey was at her side, she fell limply into his arms.

"One moment, dear," he said gently as he laid her down carefully in the armchair. The professor was down on the floor beside her in a moment, watching her fluttering eyelids.

"Dad?" she breathed. "I'm all right."

Heagey stepped quickly to his switches and threw the big one in and out again. Again came the crash cut short and the sensation of movement. And the Thing was gone. There was nothing left of it at all.

"Did you let the Thing go?" the professor reproved querulously.

"I had to," Heagey snapped. "It was a promise—for finding Sheila."

The professor was sitting on the floor, writing a check.

"Do you think you deserve this?" he said testily. He was merely trying to hide his emotion. "You won't get it until you prove it. Explain how you did this!"

Heagey dropped into a chair, looking exhausted to the limit.

"I reasoned from the things I saw Out There that this creature must be intelligent. There were buildings, machines, and leather and metal webbing. So I made models and tried to deduce its shape. Somewhere on it there must be a head and eyes. You saw how I coaxed it 'through' this 'space' of ours until the head was cut by our 'space' and the eyes could see us. Then I told it what I wanted it to do with models—just as I would explain things to you by means of drawings on a sheet of paper.

"Now do you believe there are four dimensions?" Heagey demanded by way of vengeance.

"Hm. Do you?" the professor countered.

"Four? I'm convinced there are a dozen or a thousand dimensions!"

Mugwump 4

ROBERT SILVERBERG

Here we see the predictive powers of science fiction at work. This story was written in 1959, a happy time in the long ago when it was still possible for New Yorkers to dial their telephones and not have their calls shunted into some improbable alien dimension. Thus the story, when written, was mere fantasy. Today, of course, such things happen all the time in New York—which is one reason why its author now lives in California.

Al Miller was only trying to phone the Friendly Finance Corporation to ask about an extension on his loan. It was a Murray Hill number, and he had dialed as far as MU-4 when the receiver clicked queerly and a voice said, "Come in, Operator Nine. Operator Nine, do you read me?"

Al frowned. "I didn't want the operator. There must be something wrong with my phone if——"

"Just a minute. Who *are* you?"

"I ought to ask *you* that," Al said. "What are you doing on the other end of my phone, anyway? I hadn't even finished dialing. I got as far as MU-4 and——"

"Well? You dialed MUgwump 4, and you got us. What more do you want?" A suspicious pause. "Say, you aren't Operator Nine!"

"No, I'm *not* Operator Nine, and I'm trying to dial a

114

Murray Hill number, and how about getting off the line?"

"Hold it, friend. Are you a Normal?"

Al blinked. "Yeah—yeah, I like to think so."

"So how'd you know the Number?"

"Dammit, I *didn't* know the number! I was trying to call someone, and all of a sudden the phone cut out and I got you, whoever the blazes *you* are."

"I'm the communications warden at MUgwump 4," the other said crisply. "And you're a suspicious individual. We'll have to investigate you."

The telephone emitted a sudden burping sound. Al felt as if his feet had grown roots. He could not move at all. It was awkward to be standing there at his own telephone in the privacy of his own room, as unbending as the Apollo Belvedere. Time still moved, he saw. The hand on the big clock above the phone had just shifted from 3:30 to 3:31.

Sweat rivered down his back as he struggled to put down the phone. He fought to lift his left foot. He strained to twitch his right eyelid. No go on all counts; he was frozen, all but his chest muscles—thank goodness for that. He still could breathe.

A few minutes later matters became even more awkward when his front door, which had been locked, opened abruptly. Three strangers entered. They looked oddly alike: a trio of Tweedledums, no more than five feet high, each wide through the waist, jowly of face and balding of head, each wearing an inadequate single-breasted blue-serge suit.

Al discovered he could roll his eyes. He rolled them. He wanted to apologize because his unexpected paralysis kept him from acting the proper part of a host, but his tongue would not obey. And on second thought it occurred that the little bald men might be connected in some way with that paralysis.

The reddest-faced of the three little men made an intricate gesture, and the stasis ended. Al nearly folded up as the tension that gripped him broke. He said, "Just who the deuce——"

"*We* will ask the questions. You are Al Miller?"

Al nodded.

"And obviously you are a Normal. So there has been a grave error. Mordecai, examine the telephone."

The second little man picked up the phone and calmly disemboweled it with three involved motions of his stubby hands. He frowned over the telephone's innards for a moment; then, humming tunelessly, he produced a wire clipper and severed the telephone cord.

"Hold on here," Al burst out. "You can't just rip out my phone like that! You aren't from the phone company!"

"Quiet," said the spokesman nastily. "Well, Mordecai?"

The second little man said "Probability 1:1,000,000. The cranch interval overlapped and his telephone matrix slipped. His call was piped into our wire by error, Waldemar."

"So he isn't a spy?" Waldemar asked.

"Doubtful. As you see, he's of rudimentary intelligence. His dialing our number was a statistical fluke."

"But now he knows about Us," said the third little man in a surprisingly deep voice. "I vote for demolecularization."

The other two whirled on their companion. "Always bloodthirsty, eh, Giovanni?" said Mordecai. "You'd violate the Code at the snap of a meson."

"There won't be any demolecularization while *I'm* in charge," added Waldemar.

"What do we do with him, then?" Giovanni demanded.

Mordecai said, "Freeze him and take him down to Headquarters. He's *their* problem."

"I think this has gone about as far as it's going to go," Al exploded at last. "However you three creeps got in here, you'd better get yourselves right out again, or——"

"Enough," Waldemar said. He stamped his foot. Al felt his jaws stiffen. He realized bewilderedly that he was frozen again. And frozen, this time, with his mouth gaping foolishly open.

The trip took about five minutes, and so far as Al was concerned it was one long blur. At the end of the journey the blur lifted for an instant, just enough to give Al one good glimpse of his surroundings—a residential street in what might have been Brooklyn or Queens (or Cincinnati or Detroit, he thought morbidly)—before he was hustled into the basement of a two-family house. He found himself in a windowless, brightly lit chamber cluttered with complex-looking machinery and with a dozen or so alarmingly identical little bald-headed men.

The chubbiest of the bunch glared sourly at him and asked, "Are you a spy?"

"I'm just an innocent bystander. I picked up my phone and started to dial, and all of a sudden some guy asked me if I was Operator Nine. Honest, that's all."

"Overlapping of the cranch interval," muttered Mordecai. "Slipped matrix."

"Umm. Unfortunate," the chubby one commented. "We'll have to dispose of him."

"Demolecularization is the best way," Giovanni put in immediately.

"Dispose of him *humanely*, I mean. It's revolting to think of taking the life of an inferior being. But he simply can't remain in this fourspace any longer, not if he Knows."

"But I *don't* know!" Al groaned. "I couldn't be any more mixed-up if I tried! Won't you please tell me——"

"Very well," said the pudgiest one, who seemed to be the leader. "Waldemar, tell him about Us."

Waldemar said, "You're now in the local headquarters of a secret mutant group working for the overthrow of humanity as you know it. By some accident you happened to dial our private communication exchange, MUtant 4——"

"I thought it was MUgwump 4," Al interjected.

"The code name, naturally," said Waldemar smoothly.

"To continue: you channeled into our communications network. You now know too much. Your presence in this space-time nexus jeopardizes the success of our entire movement. Therefore we are forced——"

"To demolecularize——" Giovanni began.

"Forced to dispose of you," Waldemar continued sternly. "We're humane beings—most of us—and we won't do anything that would make you suffer. But you can't stay in this area of space-time. You see our point of view, of course."

Al shook his head dimly. These little potbellied men were mutants working for the overthrow of humanity? Well, he had no reason to think they were lying to him. The world was full of little potbellied men. Maybe they were all part of the secret organization, Al thought.

"Look," he said, "I didn't *want* to dial your number, get me? It was all a big accident. But I'm a fair guy. Let me get out of here and I'll keep mum about the whole thing. You can go ahead and overthrow humanity, if that's what you want to do. I promise not to interfere in any way. If you're mutants, you ought to be able to look into my mind and see that I'm sincere——"

"We have no telepathic powers," declared the chubby leader curtly. "If we had, there would be no need for a communications network in the first place. In the second place your sincerity is not the issue. We have enemies. If you were to fall into their hands——"

"I won't say a word! Even if they stick splinters under my fingernails, I'll keep quiet!"

"No. At this stage in our campaign we can take no risks. You'll have to go. Prepare the temporal centrifuge."

Four of the little men, led by Mordecai, unveiled a complicated-looking device of the general size and shape of a concrete mixer. Waldemar and Giovanni gently shoved Al toward the machine. It came rapidly to life: dials glowed, indicator needles teetered, loud buzzes and clicks implied readiness.

Al said nervously, "What are you going to do to me?"

Waldemar explained. "This machine will hurl you forward in time. Too bad we have to rip you right out of your temporal matrix, but we've no choice. You'll be well taken care of up ahead, though. No doubt by the twenty-fifth century our kind will have taken over completely. You'll be the last of the Normals. Practically a living fossil. You'll love it. You'll be a walking museum piece."

"Assuming the machine works," Giovanni put in maliciously. "We don't really know if it does, you see."

Al gaped. They were busily strapping him to a cold copper slab in the heart of the machine. "You don't even know if it *works?*"

"Not really," Waldemar admitted. "Present theory holds that time-travel works only one way—*forward*. So we haven't been able to recover any of our test specimens and see how they reacted. Of course, they *do vanish* when the machine is turned on, so we know they must go *somewhere*."

"Oh," Al said weakly.

He was trussed in thoroughly. Experimental wriggling of his right wrist showed him that. But even if he could get loose, these weird little men would only "freeze" him and put him into the machine again.

His shoulders slumped resignedly. He wondered if anyone would miss him. The Friendly Finance Corporation certainly would. But since, in a sense, it was their fault he was in this mess now, he couldn't get very upset about that. They could always sue his estate for the three hundred dollars he owed them, if his estate were worth that much.

Nobody else was going to mind the disappearance of Albert Miller from the space-time continuum, he thought dourly. His parents were dead, he hadn't seen his one sister in fifteen years, and the girl he used to know in Topeka was married and at last report had three kids.

Still and all, he rather liked 1969. He wasn't sure how he would take to the twenty-fifth century—or the twenty-fifth century to him.

"Ready for temporal discharge," Mordecai sang out.

The chubby leader peered up at Al. "We're sorry about all this, you understand. But nothing and nobody can be allowed to stand in the way of the Cause."

"Sure," Al said. "I understand."

The concrete-mixer part of the machine began to revolve, bearing Al with it as it built up tempokinetic potential. Momentum increased alarmingly. In the background Al heard an ominous droning sound that grew louder and louder, until it drowned out everything else. His head reeled. The room and its fat little mutants went blurry. He heard a *pop!* like the sound of a breaking balloon.

It was the rupturing of the space-time continuum. Al Miller went hurtling forward along the fourspace track, head first. He shut his eyes and hoped for the best.

When the dizziness stopped, he found himself sitting in the middle of an impeccably clean, faintly yielding roadway, staring up at the wheels of vehicles swishing by overhead at phenomenal speeds. After a moment or two more, he realized they were not airborne, but simply automobiles racing along an elevated roadway made of some practically invisible substance.

So the temporal centrifuge *had* worked! Al glanced around. A crowd was collecting. A couple of hundred people had formed a big circle. They were pointing and muttering. Nobody approached closer than fifty or sixty feet.

They weren't potbellied mutants. Without exception they were all straight-backed six-footers with full heads of hair. The women were tall, too. Men and women alike were dressed in a sort of tuniclike garment made of iridescent material that constantly changed colors.

A gong began to ring, rapidly peaking in volume. Al scrambled to his feet and assayed a tentative smile.

"My name's Miller. I come from 1969. Would somebody mind telling me what year this is, and——"

He was drowned out by two hundred voices screaming

in terror. The crowd stampeded away, dashing madly in every direction, as if he were some ferocious monster. The gong continued to clang loudly. Cars hummed overhead. Suddenly Al saw a squat, beetle-shaped black vehicle coming toward him on the otherwise empty road. The car pulled up half a block away, the top sprang open, and a figure clad in what might have been a diver's suit—or a spacesuit—stepped out and advanced toward Al.

"Dozzinon murrifar volan," the armored figure called out.

"No speaka da lingo," Al replied. "I'm a stranger here."

To his dismay he saw the other draw something shaped like a weapon and point it at him. Al's hands shot immediately into the air. A globe of bluish light exuded from the broad nozzle of the gun, hung suspended for a moment, and drifted toward Al. He dodged uneasily to one side, but the globe of light followed him, descended, and wrapped itself completely around him.

It was like being on the inside of a soap bubble. He could see out, though distortedly. He touched the curving side of the globe experimentally; it was resilient and springy to the touch, but his finger did not penetrate.

He noticed with some misgiving that his bubble cage was starting to drift off the ground. It trailed a ropelike extension, which the man in the spacesuit deftly grabbed and knotted to the rear bumper of his car. He drove quickly away—with Al, bobbing in his impenetrable bubble of light, tagging willy-nilly along like a caged tiger or like a captured Gaul being dragged through the streets of Rome behind a chariot.

He got used to the irregular motion after a while and relaxed enough to be able to study his surroundings. He was passing through a remarkably antiseptic-looking city, free from refuse and dust. Towering buildings, all bright and spankingly new-looking, shot up everywhere. People goggled at him from the safety of the pedestrian walkways as he jounced past.

After about ten minutes the car halted outside an im
posing building whose facade bore the words ISTFAC
BARNOLL. Three men in spacesuits appeared from within
to flank Al's captor as a kind of honor guard. Al was borne
within.

He was nudged gently into a small room on the ground
floor. The door rolled shut behind him and seemed to join
the rest of the wall; no division line was apparent. A moment later the balloon popped open, and just in time,
too; the air had been getting quite stale inside it.

Al glanced around. A square window opened in the wall,
and three grim-faced men peered intently at him from an
adjoining cubicle. A voice from a speaker grid above Al's
head said, "Murrifar althrosk?"

"Al Miller, from the twentieth century. And it wasn't
my idea to come here, believe me."

"Durberal haznik? Quittimar? Dorbfenk?"

Al shrugged. "No parley-voo. Honest, I don't savvy."

His three interrogators conferred among themselves—
taking what seemed to Al like the needless precaution of
switching off the mike to prevent him from overhearing
their deliberations. He saw one of the men leave the observation cubicle. When he returned, some five minutes
later, he brought with him a tall, gloomy-looking man
wearing an impressive spade-shaped beard.

The mike was turned on again. Spadebeard said rum-
blingly, "How be thou hight?"

"Eh?"

"An thou reck the King's tongue, I conjure thee speak!"

Al grinned. No doubt they had fetched an expert in
ancient languages to talk to him. "Right language, but the
wrong time. I'm from the *twentieth* century. Come forward
a ways."

Spadebeard paused to change mental gears. "A thousand pardons—I mean, *sorry*. Wrong idiom. Dig me now?"

"I follow you. What year is this?"

"2431. And from whence be you?"

"You don't quite have it straight, yet. But I'm from 1969."

"And how came you hither?"

"I wish I knew," Al said. "I was just trying to phone the loan company, see . . . anyway, I got involved with these little fat guys who wanted to take over the world. Mutants, they said they were. And they decided they had to get rid of me, so they bundled me into their time machine and shot me forward. So I'm here."

"A spy of the mutated ones, eh?"

"Spy? Who said anything about being a spy? Talk about jumping to conclusions! I'm——"

"You have been sent by Them to wreak mischief among us. No transparent story of yours will deceive us. You are not the first to come to our era, you know. And you will meet the same fate the others met."

Al shook his head foggily. "Look here, you're making some big mistake. I'm not a spy for anybody. And I don't want to get involved in any war between you and the mutants——"

"The war is over. The last of the mutated ones was exterminated fifty years ago."

"Okay, then. What can you fear from me? Honest, I don't want to cause any trouble. If the mutants are wiped out, how could my spying help them?"

"No action in time and space is ever absolute. In our fourspace the mutants are eradicated—but they lurk elsewhere, waiting for their chance to enter and spread destruction."

Al's brain was swimming. "Okay, let that pass. But I'm *not* a spy. I just want to be left alone. Let me settle down here somewhere—put me on probation—show me the ropes, stake me to a few credits, or whatever you use for money here. I won't make any trouble."

"Your body teems with microorganisms of diseases long

since extinct in this world. Only the fact that we were able to confine you in a force-bubble almost as soon as you arrived here saved us from a terrible epidemic of ancient diseases."

"A couple of injections, that's all, and you can kill any bacteria on me." Al pleaded. "You're advanced people. You ought to be able to do a simple thing like that."

"And then there is the matter of your genetic structure," Spadebeard continued inexorably. "You bear genes long since eliminated from humanity as undesirable. Permitting you to remain here, breeding uncontrollably, would introduce unutterable confusion. Perhaps you carry latently the same mutant strain that cost humanity so many centuries of bloodshed!"

"No," Al protested. "Look at me. I'm six feet tall, no potbelly, a full head of hair—"

"The gene is recessive. But it crops up unexpectedly."

"I solemnly promise to control my breeding," Al declared. "I won't run around scattering my genes all over your shiny new world. That's a promise."

"Your appeal is rejected," came the inflexible reply.

Al shrugged. He knew when he was beaten. "Okay," he said wearily. "I didn't want to live in your damn century anyway. When's the execution?"

"*Execution?*" Spadebeard looked stunned. "The twentieth-century referent—yes, it is! Dove's whiskers, do you think we would—would actually—"

He couldn't get the word out. Al supplied it.

"Put me to death?"

Spadebeard's expression was sickly. He looked ready to retch. Al heard him mutter vehemently to his companions in the observation cubicle: "Gonnim def larrimog! Egfar!"

"Murrifar althrosk," suggested one of his companions.

Spadebeard, evidently reassured, nodded. He said to Al, "No doubt a barbarian like yourself *would* expect to be— to be made dead." Gulping, he went gamely on. "We have no such vindictive intention."

"Well, what *are* you going to do to me?"

"Send you across the timeline to a world where your friends the mutated ones reign supreme," Spadebeard replied. "It's the least we can do for you, spy."

The hidden door of his cell puckered open. Another space-suited figure entered, pointed a gun, and discharged a blob of blue light that drifted toward Al and rapidly englobed him. He was drawn by the trailing end out into a corridor.

It hadn't been a very sociable reception, here in the twenty-fifth century, he thought as he was tugged along the hallway. In a way he couldn't blame them. A time-traveler from the past was bound to be laden down with all sorts of germs. They couldn't risk letting him run around *breathing* at everybody. No wonder that crowd of onlookers had panicked when he opened his mouth to speak to them.

The other business, though, that of his being a spy for the mutants—he couldn't figure that out at all. If the mutants had been wiped out fifty years ago, why worry about spies now? At least his species had managed to defeat the underground organization of potbellied little men. That was comforting. He wished he could get back to 1969 if only to snap his fingers in their jowly faces and tell them that all their sinister scheming was going to come to nothing.

Where was he heading now? Spadebeard had said, *Across the timeline to a world where the mutated ones reign supreme.* Whatever across the timeline meant, Al thought.

He was ushered into an impressive laboratory room and, bubble and all, was thrust into the waiting clasps of something that looked depressingly like an electric chair. Brisk technicians bustled around, throwing switches and checking connections.

Al glanced appealingly at Spadebeard. "Will you tell me what's going on?"

"It is very difficult to express it in medieval terms," the linguist said. "The device makes use of dollibar force to transmit you through an inverse dormin vector—do I make myself clear?"

"Not very."

"Unhelpable. But you understand the concept of parallel continua at least, of course."

"No."

"Does it mean anything to you if I say that you'll be shunted across the spokes of the time-wheel to a totality that is simultaneously parallel and tangent to our four-space?"

"I get the general idea," Al said dubiously, though all he was really getting was a headache. "You might as well start shunting me, I suppose."

Spadebeard nodded and turned to a technician. "Vorstrar althrosk," he commanded.

"Murrifar."

The technician grabbed an immense toggle switch with both hands and groaningly dragged it shut. Al heard a brief whine of closing relays. Then darkness surrounded him.

Once again he found himself on a city street. But the pavement was cracked and buckled, and grass blades shot up through the neglected concrete.

A dry voice said, "All right, you. Don't sprawl there like a ninny. Get up and come along."

Al peered doubtfully up into the snout of a fair-sized pistol of enormous caliber. It was held by a short, fat, bald-headed man. Four identical companions stood near him with arms folded. They all looked very much like Mordecai, Waldemar, Giovanni, and the rest, except that these mutants were decked out in futuristic-looking costumes bright with flashy gold trim and rocket-ship insignia.

Al put up his hands. "Where am I?" he asked hesitantly.

"Earth, of course. You've just come through a dimensional gateway from the continuum of the Normals. Come along, spy. Into the van."

"But I'm *not* a spy," Al mumbled protestingly as the five little men bundled him into a blue and red car the size of a small yacht. "At least, I'm not spying on *you*. I mean——"

"Save the explanations for the Overlord" was the curt instruction.

Al huddled miserably cramped between two vigilant mutants while the others sat behind him. The van moved seemingly of its own volition and at an enormous rate. A mutant power, Al thought. After a while he said, "Could you at least tell me what year this is?"

"2431," snapped the mutant to his left.

"But that's the same year it was over *there*."

"Of course. What did you expect?"

The question floored Al. He was silent for perhaps half a mile more. Since the van had no windows, he stared morosely at his feet. Finally he asked, "How come you aren't afraid of catching my germs, then? Over back of— ah—the dimensional gateway, they kept me cooped up in a force-field all the time so I wouldn't contaminate them. But you go right ahead breathing the same air as I do."

"Do you think we fear the germs of a Normal, spy?" sneered the mutant at Al's right. "You forget that we're a superior race."

Al nodded. "Yes. I forgot about that."

The van halted suddenly and the mutant police hustled Al out, past a crowd of peering little fat men and women, and into a colossal dome of a building whose exterior was covered completely with faceted green glass. The effect was one of massive ugliness.

They ushered him into a sort of throne room presided over by a mutant fatter than the rest. The policeman gripping Al's right arm hissed, "Bow when you enter the presence of the Overlord."

Al wasn't minded to argue. He dropped to his knees along with the others. A booming voice from above rang out. "What have you brought me today?"

"A spy, your nobility."

"Another? Rise, spy."

Al rose. "Begging your nobility's pardon, I'd like to put in a word or two on my own behalf——"

"Silence!" the Overlord roared.

Al closed his mouth. The mutant drew himself up to his full height, about five feet one, and said, "The Normals have sent you across the dimensional gulf to spy on us."

"No, your nobility. They were afraid I'd spy on *them*, so they tossed me over here. In from the year 1969, you see." Briefly, he explained everything, beginning with the bollixed phone call and ending with his capture by the Overlord's men a short while ago.

The Overlord looked skeptical. "It is well known that the Normals plan to cross the dimensional gulf from their phantom world to this, the real one, and invade our civilization. You're but the latest of their advance scouts. Admit it!"

"Sorry, your nobility, but I'm not. On the other side they told me I was a spy from 1969, and now you say I'm a spy from the other dimension. But I tell you——"

"Enough!" the mutant leader thundered. "Take him away. Place him in custody. We shall decide his fate later!"

Someone else already occupied the cell into which Al was thrust. He was a lanky, sad-faced Normal who slouched forward to shake hands once the door had clanged shut.

"Thurizad manifosk," he said.

"Sorry. I don't speak that language," said Al.

The other grinned. "I understand. All right: greetings. I'm Darren Phelp. Are you a spy too?"

"No, dammit!" Al snapped. Then: "Sorry. Didn't mean to take it out on you. My name's Al Miller. Are you a native of this place?"

"Me? Dove's whiskers, what a sense of humor! Of course I'm not a native! You know as well as I do that there aren't any Normals left in this fourspace continuum."

"None at all?"

"Hasn't been one born here in centuries," Phelp said. "But you're just joking, eh? You're from Baileffod's outfit, I suppose."

"Who?"

"Baileffod. *Baileffod!* You mean you aren't? Then you must be from Higher Up!" Phelp thrust his hands sideways in some kind of gesture of respect. "Penguin's paws, Excellency, I apologize. I should have seen at once——"

"No, I'm not from your organization at all," Al said. "I don't know what you're talking about, really."

Phelp smiled cunningly. "Of *course*, Excellency! I understand completely."

"Cut that out! Why doesn't anyone ever believe me? I'm not from Baileffod and I'm not from Higher Up. I come from 1969. Do you hear me, 1969? And that's the truth."

Phelp's eyes went wide. "From the *past?*"

Al nodded. "I stumbled into the mutants in 1969, and they threw me five centuries ahead to get rid of me. Only when I arrived, I wasn't welcome, so I was shipped across the dimensional whatzis to here. Everyone thinks I'm a spy, wherever I go. What are *you* doing here?"

Phelp smiled. "Why, I *am* a spy."

"From 2431?"

"Naturally. We have to keep tabs on the mutants somehow. I came through the gateway wearing an invisibility shield, but it popped an ultrone, and I vizzed out. They jugged me last month, and I suppose I'm here for keeps."

Al rubbed thumbs tiredly against his eyeballs. "Wait a minute—how come you speak my language? On the other side they had to get a linguistics expert to talk to me."

"All spies are trained to talk English, stupid. That's the language the mutants speak here. In the real world we speak Vorkish, naturally. It's the language developed by

Normals for communication during the Mutant Wars. Your 'linguistics expert' was probably one of our top spies."

"And over here the mutants have won?"

"Completely. Three hundred years ago, in this continuum, the mutants developed a two-way time machine that enabled them to go back and forth, eliminating Normal leaders before they were born. Whereas in our world, the *real* world, two-way time-travel is impossible. That's where the continuum split begins. We Normals fought a grim war of extermination against the mutants in our four-space and finally wiped them out, despite their superior mental powers, in 2390. Clear?"

"More or less." Rather less than more, Al added privately. "So there are only mutants in this world, and only Normals in your world."

"Exactly!"

"And you're a spy from the other side."

"You've got it now! You see, even though strictly speaking this world is only a phantom, it's got some pretty real characteristics. For instance, if the mutants killed you here, you'd be dead. Permanently. So there's a lot of rivalry across the gateway; the mutants are always scheming to invade us, and vice versa. Confidentially, I don't think anything will ever come of all the scheming."

"You don't?"

"Nah," Phelp said. "The way things stand now, each side has a perfectly good enemy just beyond reach. But actually going to war would be messy, while relaxing our guard and slipping into peace would foul up our economy. So we keep sending spies back and forth and prepare for war. It's a nice system, except when you happen to get caught, like me."

"What'll happen to you?"

Phelp shrugged. "They may let me rot here for a few decades. Or they might decide to condition me and send me back as a spy for *them*. Tiger tails, who knows?"

"Would you change sides like that?"

"I wouldn't have any choice—not after I was conditioned," Phelp said. "But I don't worry much about it. It's a risk I knew about when I signed on for spy duty."

Al shuddered. It was beyond him how someone could *voluntarily* let himself get involved in this game of dimension-shifting and mutant-battling. But it takes all sorts to make a continuum, he decided.

Half an hour later three rotund mutant police came to fetch him. They marched him downstairs and into a bare, ugly little room where a battery of interrogators quizzed him for better than an hour. He stuck to his story, throughout everything, until at last they indicated they were through with him. He spent the next two hours in a drafty cell, by himself, until finally a gaudily robed mutant unlocked the door and said, "The Overlord wishes to see you."

The Overlord looked worried. He leaned forward on his throne, fist digging into his fleshy chin. In his booming voice—Al realized suddenly that it was artificially amplified—the Overlord rumbled, "Miller, you're a *problem*."

"I'm sorry, your nobil——"

"*Quiet!* I'll do the talking."

Al did not reply.

The Overlord went on, "We've checked your story inside and out and confirmed it with one of our spies on the other side of the gate. You really *are* from 1969, or thereabouts. What can we do with you? Generally speaking, when we catch a Normal snooping around here, we psychocondition him and send him back across the gateway to spy for us. But we can't do that to you, because you don't belong on the other side, and they've already tossed you out once. On the other hand, we can't keep you here, maintaining you forever at state expense. And it wouldn't be civilized to kill you, would it?"

"No, your nobil——"

"*Silence!*"

Al gulped. The Overlord glowered at him and continued thinking out loud. "I suppose we could perform experiments on you, though. You must be a walking laboratory of Normal microorganisms that we could synthesize and fire through the gateway when we invade their fourspace. Yes, by the Grome, then you'd be useful to our cause! Zechariah?"

"Yes, Nobility?" A ribbon-bedecked guardsman snapped to attention.

"Take this Normal to the Biological Laboratories for examination. I'll have further instructions as soon as—"

Al heard a peculiar whanging noise from the back of the throne room. The Overlord appeared to freeze on his throne. Turning, Al saw a band of determined-looking Normals come bursting in, led by Darren Phelp.

"*There* you are!" Phelp cried. "I've been looking all over for you!" He was waving a peculiar needle-nozzled gun.

"What's going on?" Al asked.

Phelp grinned. "The Invasion! It came, after all! Our troops are pouring through the gateway armed with these freezer guns. They immobilize any mutant who gets in the way of the field."

"When—when did all this happen?"

"It started two hours ago. We've captured the entire city! Come on, will you? Whiskers, there's no time to waste!"

"Where am I supposed to go?"

Phelp smiled. "To the nearest dimensional lab, of course. We're going to send you back home."

A dozen triumphant Normals stood in a tense knot around Al in the laboratory. From outside came the sound of jubilant singing. The Invasion was a howling success.

As Phelp had explained it, the victory was due to the

recent invention of a kind of time-barrier projector. The projector had cut off all contact between the mutant world and its own future, preventing time-traveling mutant scouts from getting back to 2431 with news of the Invasion. Thus two-way travel, the great mutant advantage, was nullified, and the success of the surprise attack was made possible.

Al listened to this explanation with minimal interest. He barely understood every third word, and in any event his main concern was in getting home.

He was strapped into a streamlined and much modified version of the temporal centrifuge that had originally hurled him into 2431. Phelp explained things to him.

"You see here, we set the machine for 1969. What day was it when you left?"

"Ah—October tenth. Around three thirty in the afternoon."

"Make the setting, Frozz." Phelp nodded. "You'll be shunted back along the timeline. Of course, you'll land in this continuum, since in our world there's no such thing as pastward time-travel. But once you reach your own time, all you do is activate this small transdimensional generator, and you'll be hurled across safe and sound into the very day you left, in your own fourspace."

"You can't know how much I appreciate all this," Al said warmly. He felt a pleasant glow of love for all mankind, for the first time since his unhappy phone call. At last someone was taking sympathetic interest in his plight. At last he was on his way home, back to the relative sanity of 1969 where he could start forgetting this entire nightmarish jaunt. Mutants and Normals and spies and time machines——

"You'd better get going," Phelp said. "We have to get the occupation under way here."

"Sure," Al agreed. "Don't let me hold you up. I can't wait to get going—no offense intended."

"And remember—soon as your surroundings look familiar, jab the activator button on this generator. Otherwise you'll slither into an interspace where we couldn't answer for the consequences."

Al nodded tensely. "I won't forget."

"I hope not. Ready?"

"Ready."

Someone threw a switch. Al began to spin. He heard the popping sound that was the rupturing of the temporal matrix. Like a cork shot from a champagne bottle, Al arched out backward through time, heading for 1969.

He woke in his own room on Twenty-third Street. His head hurt. His mind was full of phrases like temporal centrifuge and transdimensional generator.

He picked himself off the floor and rubbed his head.

Wow, he thought. It must have been a sudden fainting spell. And now his head was full of nonsense.

Going to the sideboard, he pulled out the half-empty bourbon bottle and measured off a few fingers' worth. After the drink, his nerves felt steadier. His mind was still cluttered with inexplicable thoughts and images. Sinister little fat men and complex machines, gleaming roadways and men in fancy tunics.

A bad dream, he thought.

Then he remembered. It wasn't any dream. He had actually taken the round trip into 2431, returning by way of some other continuum. He had pressed the generator button at the proper time, and now here he was, safe and sound. No longer the football of a bunch of different factions. Home in his own snug little fourspace, or whatever it was.

He frowned. He recalled that Mordecai had severed the telephone wire. But the phone looked intact now. Maybe it had been fixed while he was gone. He picked it up. Unless he got that loan extension today, he was cooked.

There was no need for him to look up the number of the

Friendly Finance Corporation; he knew it well enough. He began to dial. MUrray Hill 4—

The receiver clicked queerly. A voice said, "Come in, Operator Nine. Operator Nine, do you read me?"

Al's jaw sagged in horror. This is where I came in, he thought wildly. He struggled to put down the phone. But his muscles would not respond. It would be easier to bend the sun in its orbit than to break the path of the continuum. He heard his own voice say, "I didn't want the operator. There must be something wrong with my phone if——"

"Just a minute. Who *are* you?"

Al fought to break the contact. But he was hemmed away in a small corner of his mind while his voice went on, "I ought to ask *you* that. What are you doing on the other end of my phone, anyway? I hadn't even finished dialing. I got as far as MU-4 and. . . ."

Inwardly Al wanted to scream. No scream would come. In this continuum the past (his future) was immutable. He was caught on the track, and there was no escape. None whatever. And, he realized glumly, there never would be.

The Worlds of If

STANLEY G. WEINBAUM

Stanley Weinbaum made his debut as a writer in 1934 with a delightful, lively story called "A Martian Odyssey," which immediately established him as one of science fiction's most entertaining and imaginative creators. In the months that followed he amazed and amused s-f readers with a host of other stories, notably a series of comic tales relating the exploits of the not-so-mad mad scientist, Haskel van Manderpootz; magazines received bushels of letters demanding still more Weinbaum, and editors did their best to get it, but the supply was suddenly and tragically cut off in December, 1935, when this gifted young writer died at the age of thirty-three. Here, in one of the van Manderpootz stories of dimension-hopping, we can see the cleverness and charm that brought Weinbaum his brief, spectacular period of fame.

I stopped on the way to the Staten Island Airport to call up, and that was a mistake, doubtless, since I had a chance of making it otherwise. But the office was affable. "We'll hold the ship five minutes for you," the clerk said. "That's the best we can do."

So I rushed back to my taxi, and we spun off to the third level and sped across the Staten Island Bridge like a comet treading a steel rainbow. I had to be in Moscow by evening, by eight o'clock, in fact, for the opening of bids on the Ural

Tunnel. The Government required the personal presence of an agent of each bidder, but the firm should have known better than to send me, Dixon Wells, even though the N. J. Wells Corporation is, so to speak, my father. I have a— well, an undeserved reputation for being late to everything; something always comes up to prevent me from getting anywhere on time. It's never my fault; this time it was a chance encounter with my old physics professor, old Haskel van Manderpootz. I couldn't very well just say hello and good-bye to him; I'd been a favorite of his back in the college days of 2014.

I missed the airliner, of course. I was still on the Staten Bridge when I heard the roar of the catapult and the Soviet rocket *Baikal* hummed over us like a tracer bullet with a long tail of flame.

We got the contract anyway; the firm wired our man in Beirut, and he flew to Moscow, but it didn't help my reputation. However, I felt a great deal better when I saw the evening papers; the *Baikal*, flying at the north edge of the eastbound lane to avoid a storm, had locked wings with a British fruitship and all but a hundred of her five hundred passengers were lost. I had almost become "the late Mr. Wells" in a grimmer sense.

I'd made an engagement for the following week with old van Manderpootz. It seems he'd transferred to N.Y.U. as head of the Department of Newer Physics—that is, of Relativity. He deserved it; the old chap was a genius if ever there was one, and even now, eight years out of college, I remember more from his course than from half a dozen calculus, steam and gas, mechanics, and other hazards on the path to an engineer's education. So on Tuesday night I dropped in an hour or so late, to tell the truth, since I'd forgotten about the engagement until mid-evening.

He was reading in a room as disorderly as ever. "Humph!" he grunted. "Time changes everything but habit,

I see. You were a good student, Dick, but I seem to recall that you always arrived in class toward the middle of the lecture."

"I had a course in East Hall just before," I explained. "I couldn't seem to make it in time."

"Well, it's time you learned to be on time," he growled. Then his eyes twinkled. "Time!" he ejaculated. "The most fascinating word in the language. Here we've used it five times (there goes the sixth time—and the seventh!) in the first minute of conversation; each of us understands the other, yet science is just beginning to learn its meaning. Science? I mean that *I* am beginning to learn."

I sat down. "You and science are synonymous," I grinned. "Aren't you one of the world's outstanding physicists?"

"One of them!" he snorted. "*One* of them, eh! And who are the others?"

"Oh, Corveille and Hastings and Shrimski——"

"Bah! Would you mention them in the same breath with the name of van Manderpootz? A pack of jackals, eating the crumbs of ideas that drop from my feast of thoughts! Had you gone back into the last century, now—had you mentioned Einstein and de Sitter—there, perhaps, are names worthy to rank with (or just below) van Manderpootz!"

I grinned again in amusement. "Einstein was considered pretty good, wasn't he?" I remarked. "After all, he was the first to tie time and space to the laboratory. Before him they were just philosophical concepts."

"He didn't!" rasped the professor. "Perhaps, in a dim primitive fashion, he showed the way, but I—I, van Manderpootz—am the first to seize time, drag it into my laboratory, and perform an experiment on it."

"Indeed? And what sort of experiment?"

"What experiment, other than simple measurement, is it possible to perform?" he snapped.

"Why—I don't know. To travel in it?"

"Exactly."

"Like these time-machines that are so popular in the current magazines? To go into the future or the past?"

"Bah! Many bahs! The future or the past—pfui! It needs no van Manderpootz to see the fallacy in that. Einstein showed us that much."

"How? It's conceivable, isn't it?"

"Conceivable? And you, Dixon Wells, studied under van Manderpootz!" He grew red with emotion, then grimly calm. "Listen to me. You know how time varies with the speed of a system—Einstein's relativity."

"Yes."

"Very well. Now suppose then that the great engineer Dixon Wells invents a machine capable of traveling very fast, enormously fast, nine-tenths as fast as light. Do you follow? Good. You then fuel this miracle ship for a little jaunt of a half-million miles, which, since mass (and with it inertia) increases according to the Einstein formula with increasing speed, takes all the fuel in the world. But you solve that. You use atomic energy. Then, since at nine-tenths light-speed, your ship weighs about as much as the sun, you disintegrate North America to give you sufficient motive power. You start off at that speed, a hundred and sixty-eight thousand miles per second, and you travel for two hundred and four thousand miles. The acceleration has now crushed you to death, but you have penetrated the future." He paused, grinning sardonically. "Haven't you?"

"Yes."

"And how far?"

I hesitated.

"Use your Einstein formula!" he screeched. "How far? I'll tell you. *One second!*" He grinned triumphantly. "That's how possible it is to travel into the future. And as for the past—in the first place, you'd have to exceed light-speed, which immediately entails the use of more than an infinite number of horsepowers. We'll assume that the great engineer Dixon Wells solves that little problem, too, even though the energy output of the whole universe is not an infinite number of horsepowers. Then he applies this more than infinite power to travel at two hundred and four thousand miles per second for *ten* seconds. He has then penetrated the past. How far?"

Again I hesitated.

"I'll tell you. *One second!*" He glared at me. "Now all you have to do is to design such a machine, and then van Manderpootz will admit the possibility of traveling into the future—for a limited number of seconds. As for the past, I have just explained that all the energy in the universe is insufficient for that."

"But," I stammered, "you just said that you——"

"I did not say anything about traveling into either future or past, which I have just demonstrated to you to be impossible—a practical impossibility in the one case and an absolute one in the other."

"Then how do you travel in time?"

"Not even van Manderpootz can perform the impossible," said the professor, now faintly jovial. He tapped a thick pad of typewriter paper on the table beside him. "See, Dick, this is the world, the universe." He swept a finger down it. "It is long in time, and"—sweeping his hand across it—"it is broad in space, but"—now jabbing his finger against its center—"it is very thin in the fourth dimension. Van Manderpootz takes always the shortest, the most logical course. I do not travel along time, into past or future. No. Me, I travel across time, sideways!"

I gulped. "Sideways into time! What's there?"

"What would naturally be there?" he snorted. "Ahead is the future; behind is the past. Those are real, the worlds of past and future. What worlds are neither past nor future, but contemporary and yet—extemporal—existing, as it were, in time parallel to our time?"

I shook my head.

"Idiot!" he snapped. "The conditional worlds, of course! The worlds of 'if.' Ahead are the worlds to be; behind are the worlds that were; to either side are the worlds that might have been—the worlds of 'if'!"

"Eh?" I was puzzled. "Do you mean that you can see what will happen if I do such and such?"

"No!" he snorted. "My machine does not reveal the past nor predict the future. It will show, as I told you, the conditional worlds. You might express it by 'if I had done such and such, so and so would have happened.' The worlds of the subjunctive mode."

"Now how the devil does it do that?"

"Simple, for van Manderpootz! I use polarized light, polarized not in the horizontal or vertical planes, but in the direction of the fourth dimension—an easy matter. One uses Iceland spar under colossal pressures, that is all. And since the worlds are very thin in the direction of the fourth dimension, the thickness of a single light wave, though it be but millionths of an inch, is sufficient. A considerable improvement over time-traveling in past or future, with its impossible velocities and ridiculous distances!"

"But—are those—worlds of 'if'—real?"

"Real? What is real? They are real, perhaps, in the sense that two is a real number as opposed to the square root of minus two, which is imaginary. They are the worlds that would have been *if*. Do you see?"

I nodded. "Dimly. You could see, for instance, what New York would have been like if England had won the Revolution instead of the Colonies."

"That's the principle, true enough, but you couldn't see that on the machine. Part of it, you see, is a Horsten psychomat (stolen from one of *my* ideas, by the way), and you, the user, become part of the device. Your own mind is necessary to furnish the background. For instance, if George Washington could have used the mechanism after the signing of peace, he could have seen what you suggest. We can't. You can't even see what would have happened if I hadn't invented the thing, but *I* can. Do you understand?"

"Of course. You mean the background has to rest in the past experiences of the user."

"You're growing brilliant," he scoffed. "Yes. The device will show ten hours of what would have happened *if*—condensed, of course, as in a movie, to half an hour's actual time."

"Say, that sounds interesting!"

"You'd like to see it? Is there anything you'd like to find out? Any choice you'd alter?"

"I'll say—a thousand of 'em. I'd like to know what would have happened if I'd sold out my stocks in 2009 instead of '10. I was a millionaire in my own right then, but I was a little—well, a little late in liquidating."

"As usual," remarked van Manderpootz. "Let's go over to the laboratory then."

The professor's quarters were but a block from the campus. He ushered me into the Physics Building and thence into his own research laboratory, much like the one I had visited during my courses under him. The device—he called it his "subjunctivisor," since it operated in hypothetical worlds—occupied the entire center table. Most of it was merely a Horsten psychomat, but glittering crystalline and glassy was the prism of Iceland spar, the polarizing agent that was the heart of the instrument.

Van Manderpootz pointed to the headpiece. "Put it on," he said, and I sat staring at the screen of the psychomat. I suppose everyone is familiar with the Horsten psychomat; it was as much a fad a few years ago as the ouija board a century back. Yet it isn't just a toy; sometimes, much as the ouija board, it's a real aid to memory. A maze of vague and colored shadows is caused to drift slowly across the screen, and one watches them, meanwhile visualizing whatever scene or circumstances he is trying to remember. He turns a knob that alters the arrangement of lights and shadows, and when, by chance, the design corresponds to his mental picture—presto! There is his scene re-created under his eyes. Of course his own mind adds the details. All the screen actually shows are these tinted blobs of light and shadow, but the thing can be amazingly real. I've seen occasions when I could have sworn the psychomat showed pictures almost as sharp and detailed as reality itself; the illusion is sometimes as startling as that.

Van Manderpootz switched on the light, and the play of shadows began. "Now recall the circumstances of, say, a half year after the market crash. Turn the knob until the picture clears, then stop. At that point I direct the light of the subjunctivisor upon the screen, and you have nothing to do but watch."

I did as directed. Momentary pictures formed and vanished. The inchoate sounds of the device hummed like distant voices, but without the added suggestion of the picture, they meant nothing. My own face flashed and dissolved, and then, finally, I had it. There was a picture of myself sitting in an ill-defined room; that was all. I released the knob and gestured.

A click followed. The light dimmed, then brightened. The picture cleared, and amazingly, another figure emerged, a woman. I recognized her; it was Whimsy White, erstwhile star of television and premiere of the *Vision Varieties of '09*. She was changed on that picture, but I recognized her.

I'll say I did! I'd been trailing her all through the boom years of '07 to '10, trying to marry her, while old N. J. raved and ranted and threatened to leave everything to the Society for Rehabilitation of the Gobi Desert. I think those threats were what kept her from accepting me, but after I took my own money and ran it up to a couple of million in that crazy market of '08 and '09, she softened.

Temporarily, that is. When the crash of the spring of '10

came and bounced me back on my father and into the firm of N. J. Wells, her favor dropped a dozen points to the market's one. In February we were engaged; in April we were hardly speaking. In May they sold me out. I'd been late again.

And now, there she was on the psychomat screen, obviously plumping out and not nearly so pretty as memory had pictured her. She was staring at me with an expression of enmity, and I was glaring back. The buzzes became voices.

"You nitwit!" she snapped. "You can't bury me out here. I want to go back to New York, where there's a little life. I'm bored with you and your golf."

"And I'm bored with you and your whole dizzy crowd."

"At least they're *alive.* You're a walking corpse. Just because you were lucky enough to gamble yourself into the money, you think you're a tin god."

"Well, I *don't* think you're Cleopatra! Those friends of yours—they trail after you because you give parties and spend money—*my* money."

"Better than spending it to knock a white walnut along a mountainside!"

"Indeed? You ought to try it, Marie." (That was her real name.) "It might help your figure—though I doubt if anything could!"

She glared in rage and—well, that was a painful half hour. I won't give all the details, but I was glad when the screen dissolved into meaningless colored clouds.

"Whew!" I said, staring at van Manderpootz, who had been reading.

"You liked it?"

"Liked it! Say, I guess I was lucky to be cleaned out. I won't regret it from now on."

"That," said the professor grandly, "is van Manderpootz's great contribution to human happiness. 'Of all sad words of tongue or pen, the saddest are these: It might

have been!' True no longer, my friend Dick. Van Manderpootz has shown that the proper reading is, 'It might have
been—worse!' "

It was very late when I returned home and as a result,
very late when I rose and equally late when I got to the
office. My father was unnecessarily worked up about it, but
he exaggerated when he said I'd never been on time. He
forgets the occasions when he's awakened me and dragged
me down with him. Nor was it necessary to refer so sarcas-
tically to my missing the *Baikal;* I reminded him of the
wrecking of the liner, and he responded very heartlessly
that if I'd been aboard, the rocket would have been late,
and so would have missed colliding with the British
fruitship. It was likewise superfluous for him to mention
that when he and I had tried to snatch a few weeks of
golfing in the mountains, even the spring had been late.
I had nothing to do with that.

"Dixon," he concluded, "you have no conception whatever of time. None whatever."

The conversation with van Manderpootz recurred to me.
I was impelled to ask, "And have you, sir?"

"I have," he said grimly. "I most assuredly have. Time,"
he said oracularly, "is money."

You can't argue with a viewpoint like that.

But those aspersions of his rankled, especially that about
the *Baikal*. Tardy I might be, but it was hardly conceivable
that my presence aboard the rocket could have averted the
catastrophe. It irritated me; in a way it made me responsible for the deaths of those unrescued hundreds among
the passengers and crew, and I didn't like the thought.

Of course, if they'd waited an extra five minutes for me,
or if I'd been on time and they'd left on schedule instead
of five minutes late, or if—*if!*

If! The word called up van Manderpootz and his subjunctivisor—the worlds of "if," the weird, unreal worlds

that existed beside reality, neither past nor future, but contemporary, yet extemporal. Somewhere among their ghostly
infinities existed one that represented the world that would
have been had I made the liner. I had only to call up Haskel van Manderpootz, make an appointment, and then find
out.

Yet it wasn't an easy decision. Suppose—just suppose
that I found myself responsible—not legally responsible,
certainly; there'd be no question of criminal negligence or
anything of that sort—not even morally responsible, because I couldn't possibly have anticipated that my presence
or absence could weigh so heavily in the scales of life and
death, nor could I have known in which direction the
scales would tip. Just—responsible; that was all. Yet I
hated to find out.

I hated equally not finding out. Uncertainty has its
pangs, too, quite as painful as those of remorse. It might
be less nerve-racking to know myself responsible than to
wonder, to waste thoughts in vain doubts and futile re-
proaches. So I seized the visiphone, dialed the number of
the university, and at length gazed on the broad, humorous, intelligent features of van Manderpootz, dragged from
a morning lecture by my call.

I was all but prompt for the appointment the following
evening and might actually have been on time but for an
unreasonable traffic officer who insisted on booking me for
speeding. At any rate, van Manderpootz was impressed.

"Well!" he rumbled. "I almost missed you, Dixon. I was
just going over to the club, since I didn't expect you for
an hour. You're only ten minutes late."

I ignored this. "Professor, I want to use your—uh—your
subjunctivisor."

"Eh? Oh, yes. You're lucky, then. I was just about to dismantle it."

"Dismantle it! Why?"

"It has served its purpose. It has given birth to an idea far more important than itself. I shall need the space it occupies."

"But what *is* the idea, if it's not too presumptuous of me to ask?"

"It is not too presumptuous. You and the world which awaits it so eagerly may both know, but you hear it from the lips of the author. It is nothing less than the autobiography of van Manderpootz!" He paused impressively.

I gaped. "Your autobiography?"

"Yes. The world, though perhaps unaware, is crying for it. I shall detail my life, my work. I shall reveal myself as the man responsible for the three years' duration of the Pacific War of 2004."

"You?"

"None other. Had I not been a loyal Netherlands subject at that time, and therefore neutral, the forces of Asia would have been crushed in three months instead of three years. The subjunctivisor tells me so; I would have invented a calculator to forecast the chances of every engagement; van Manderpootz would have removed the hit-or-miss element in the conduct of war." He frowned solemnly. "There is my idea. The autobiography of van Manderpootz. What do you think of it?"

I recovered my thoughts. "It's—uh—it's colossal!" I said vehemently. "I'll buy a copy myself. Several copies. I'll send 'em to my friends."

"I," said van Manderpootz expansively, "shall autograph your copy for you. It will be priceless. I shall write in some fitting phrase, perhaps something like *Magnificus sed non superbus.* 'Great but not proud!' That well describes van Manderpootz, who despite his greatness is simple, modest, and unassuming. Don't you agree?"

"Perfectly! A very apt description of you. But—couldn't I see your subjunctivisor before it's dismantled to make way for the greater work?"

"Ah! You wish to find out something?"

"Yes, professor. Do you remember the *Baikal* disaster of a week or two ago? I was to have taken that liner to Moscow. I just missed it." I related the circumstances.

"Humph!" he grunted. "You wish to discover what would have happened had you caught it, eh? Well, I see several possibilities. Among the worlds of 'if' is the one that would have been real if you have been on time, the one that depended on the vessel waiting for your actual arrival, and the one that hung on your arriving within the five minutes they actually waited. In which are you interested?"

"Oh—the last one." That seemed the likeliest. After all, it was too much to expect that Dixon Wells could ever be on time, and as to the second possibility—well, they *hadn't* waited for me, and that in a way removed the weight of responsibility.

"Come on," rumbled van Manderpootz. I followed him across to the Physics Building and into his littered laboratory. The device still stood on the table, and I took my place before it, staring at the screen of the Horsten psychomat. The clouds wavered and shifted as I sought to impress my memories on their suggestive shapes, to read into them some picture of that vanished morning.

Then I had it. I made out the vista from the Staten Bridge and was speeding across the giant span toward the airport. I waved a signal to van Manderpootz, the thing clicked, and the subjunctivisor was on.

The grassless clay of the field appeared. It is a curious thing about the psychomat that you see only through the eyes of your image on the screen. It lends a strange reality to the working of the toy; I suppose a sort of self-hypnosis is partly responsible.

I was rushing over the ground toward the glittering, silver-winged projectile that was the *Baikal*. A glowering officer waved me on, and I dashed up the slant of the gangplank and into the ship; the port dropped and I heard a long "Whew!" of relief.

"Sit down!" barked the officer, gesturing toward an unoccupied seat. I fell into it; the ship quivered under the thrust of the catapult, grated harshly into motion, and then was flung bodily into the air. The blasts roared instantly, then settled to a more muffled throbbing, and I watched Staten Island drop down and slide back beneath me. The giant rocket was under way.

"Whew!" I breathed again. "Made it!" I caught an amused glance from my right. I was in an aisle seat; there was no one to my left, so I turned to the eyes that had flashed, glanced, and froze staring.

It was a girl. Perhaps she wasn't actually as lovely as she looked to me; after all, I was seeing her through the half-visionary screen of a psychomat. I've told myself since that she *couldn't* have been as pretty as she seemed, that it was due to my own imagination, filling in the details. I don't know; I remember only that I stared at curiously lovely silver-blue eyes and velvety brown hair and a small amused mouth and an impudent nose. I kept staring until she flushed.

"I'm sorry," I said quickly. "I—was startled."

There's a friendly atmosphere aboard a transoceanic rocket. The passengers are forced into a crowded intimacy for anywhere from seven to twelve hours, and there isn't much room for moving about. Generally, one strikes up an acquaintance with his neighbors; introductions aren't at all necessary, and the custom is simply to speak to anybody you choose—something like an all-day trip on the railroad trains of the last century, I suppose. You make friends for the duration of the journey, and then, nine times out of ten, you never hear of your traveling companions again.

The girl smiled. "Are you the individual responsible for the delay in starting?"

I admitted it. "I seem to be chronically late. Even watches lose time as soon as I wear them."

She laughed. "Your responsibilities can't be very heavy."

Well, they weren't of course, though it's surprising how

many clubs, caddies, and chorus girls have depended on me at various times for appreciable portions of their incomes. But somehow I didn't feel like mentioning those things to the silvery-eyed girl.

We talked. Her name, it developed, was Joanna Caldwell, and she was going as far as Paris. She was an artist, or hoped to be one day, and of course there is no place in the world that can supply both training and inspiration like Paris. So it was there she was bound for a year of study, and despite her demurely humorous lips and laughing eyes, I could see that the business was of vast importance to her. I gathered that she had worked hard for the year in Paris, had scraped and saved for three years as fashion illustrator for some woman's magazine, though she couldn't have been many months over twenty-one. Her painting meant a great deal to her, and I could understand it. I'd felt that way about polo once.

So you see, we were sympathetic spirits from the beginning. I knew that she liked me, and it was obvious that she didn't connect Dixon Wells with the N. J. Wells Corporation. And as for me—well, after that first glance into her cool silver eyes, I simply didn't care to look anywhere else. The hours seemed to drip away like minutes while I watched her.

You know how those things go. Suddenly I was calling her Joanna and she was calling me Dick, and it seemed as if we'd been doing just that all our lives. I'd decided to stop over in Paris on my way back from Moscow, and I'd secured her promise to let me see her. She was different, I tell you; she was nothing like the calculating Whimsy White, and still less like the dancing, simpering, giddy youngsters one meets around at social affairs. She was just Joanna, cool and humorous, yet sympathetic and serious, and as pretty as a Majolica figurine.

We could scarcely realize it when the steward passed along to take orders for luncheon. Four hours out? It seemed like forty minutes. And we had a pleasant feeling of intimacy in the discovery that both of us liked lobster salad and detested oysters. It was another bond; I told her whimsically that it was an omen, nor did she object to considering it so.

Afterward we walked along the narrow aisle to the glassed-in observation room up forward. It was almost too crowded for entry, but we didn't mind that at all, as it forced us to sit very close together. We stayed long after both of us had begun to notice the stuffiness of the air.

It was just after we had returned to our seats that the catastrophe occurred. There was no warning save a sudden lurch, the result, I suppose, of the pilot's futile last-minute attempt to swerve—just that and then a grinding crash and a terrible sensation of spinning, and after that a chorus of shrieks that were like the sounds of battle.

It was battle. Five hundred people were picking themselves up from the floor, were trampling each other, milling around, being cast helplessly down as the great rocket-plane, its left wing but a broken stub, circled downward toward the Atlantic.

The shouts of officers sounded, and a loudspeaker blared. "Be calm," it kept repeating, and then, "There has been a collision. We have contacted a surface ship. There is no danger. There is no danger—"

I struggled up from the debris of shattered seats. Joanna was gone; just as I found her crumpled between the rows, the ship struck the water with a jar that set everything crashing again. The speaker blared, "Put on the cork belts under the seats. The lifebelts are under the seats."

I dragged a belt loose and snapped it around Joanna, then donned one myself. The crowd was surging forward now, and the tail end of the ship began to drop. There was water behind us, sloshing in the darkness as the lights went out. An officer came sliding by, stooped, and fastened a belt about an unconscious woman ahead of us. "You all right?" he yelled and passed on without waiting for an answer.

The speaker must have been cut on to a battery circuit.

"And get as far away as possible," it ordered suddenly. "Jump from the forward port and get as far away as possible. A ship is standing by. You will be picked up. Jump from the—" It went dead again.

I got Joanna untangled from the wreckage. She was pale; her silvery eyes were closed. I started dragging her slowly and painfully toward the forward port, and the slant of the floor increased until it was like the slide of a ski jump. The officer passed again. "Can you handle her?" he asked and again dashed away.

I was getting there. The crowd around the port looked smaller, or was it simply huddling closer? Then suddenly a wail of fear and despair went up, and there was a roar of water. The observation-room walls had given. I saw the green surge of waves, and a billowing deluge rushed down upon us. I had been late again.

That was all. I raised shocked and frightened eyes from the subjunctivisor to face van Manderpootz, who was scribbling on the edge of the table.

"Well?" he asked.

I shuddered. "Horrible!" I murmured. "We—I guess we wouldn't have been among the survivors."

"We, eh? We?" His eyes twinkled.

I did not enlighten him. I thanked him, bade him good night, and went dolorously home.

Even my father noticed something queer about me. The day I got to the office only five minutes late, he called me in for some anxious questioning as to my health. I couldn't tell him anything, of course. How could I explain that I'd been late once too often and had fallen in love with a girl two weeks after she was dead?

The thought drove me nearly crazy. Joanna! Joanna with her silvery eyes now lay somewhere at the bottom of the Atlantic. I went around half dazed, scarcely speaking. One night I actually lacked the energy to go home and sat smoking in my father's big overstuffed chair in his private office until I finally dozed off. The next morning, when old N. J. entered and found me there before him, he turned pale as paper, staggered, and gasped, "My heart!" It took a lot of explaining to convince him that I wasn't early at the office but just very late going home.

At last I felt that I couldn't stand it. I had to do something—anything at all. I thought finally of the subjunctivisor. I could see—yes, I could see what would have transpired if the ship hadn't been wrecked! I could trace out that weird, unreal romance hidden somewhere in the worlds of "if." I could, perhaps, wring a somber, vicarious joy from the things that might have been. I could see Joanna once more!

It was late afternoon when I rushed over to van Manderpootz's quarters. He wasn't there; I encountered him finally in the hall of the Physics Building.

"Dick!" he exclaimed. "Are you sick?"

"Sick? No. Not physically. Professor, I've got to use your subjunctivisor again. I've *got* to!"

"Eh? Oh—that toy. You're too late, Dick. I've dismantled it. I have a better use for the space."

I gave a miserable groan and was tempted to damn the autobiography of the great van Manderpootz. A gleam of sympathy showed in his eyes, and he took my arm, dragging me into the little office adjoining his laboratory.

"Tell me," he commanded.

I did. I guess I made the tragedy plain enough, for his heavy brows knit in a frown of pity. "Not even van Manderpootz can bring back the dead," he murmured. "I'm sorry, Dick. Take your mind from the affair. Even were my subjunctivisor available, I wouldn't permit you to use it. That would be but to turn the knife in the wound." He paused. "Find something else to occupy your mind. Do as van Manderpootz does. Find forgetfulness in work."

"Yes," I responded dully. "But who'd want to read my autobiography? That's all right for you."

"Autobiography? Oh! I remember. No, I have abandoned

that. History itself will record the life and works of van Manderpootz. Now I am engaged in a far grander project."

"Indeed?" I was utterly, gloomily disinterested.

"Yes. Gogli has been here, Gogli the sculptor. He is to make a bust of me. What better legacy can I leave to the world than a bust of van Manderpootz, sculptured from life? Perhaps I shall present it to the city, perhaps to the university. I would have given it to the Royal Society if they had been a little more receptive, if they—if—*if!*" The last in a shout.

"Huh?"

"*If!*" cried van Manderpootz. "What you saw in the subjunctivisor was what would have happened *if* you had caught the ship!"

"I know that."

"But something quite different might really have happened! Don't you see? She—she— Where are those old newspapers?"

He was pawing through a pile of them. He flourished one finally. "Here! Here are the survivors!"

Like letters of flame, Joanna Caldwell's name leaped out at me. There was even a little paragraph about it, as I saw once my reeling brain permitted me to read:

> At least a score of survivors owe their lives to the bravery of twenty-eight-year-old Navigator Orris Hope, who patrolled both aisles during the panic, lacing lifebelts on the injured and helpless and carrying many to the port. He remained on the sinking liner until the last, finally fighting his way to the surface through the broken walls of the observation room. Among those who owe their lives to the young officer are: Patrick Owensby, New York City; Mrs. Campbell Warren, Boston; Miss Joanna Caldwell, New York City. . . .

I suppose my shout of joy was heard over in the Administration Building, blocks away. I didn't care; if van

Manderpootz hadn't been armored in stubby whiskers, I'd have kissed him. Perhaps I did anyway; I can't be sure of my actions during those chaotic minutes in the professor's tiny office.

At last I calmed. "I can look her up!" I gloated. "She must have landed with the other survivors, and they were all on that British tramp freighter the *Osgood*, that docked here last week. She must be in New York—and if she's gone over to Paris, I'll find out and follow her!"

Well, it's a queer ending. She was in New York, but— you see, Dixon Wells had, so to speak, known Joanna Caldwell by means of the professor's subjunctivisor, but Joanna had never known Dixon Wells. What the ending might have been if—*if*— But it wasn't; she had married Orris Hope, the young officer who had rescued her. I was late again.

Disappearing Act

ALFRED BESTER

It is much too long since the byline of Alfred
Bester last appeared on a new science-fiction
story. In the 1950's he shot past like a glittering
comet, leaving behind a score of dazzling short
stories and two classic novels, *The Demolished
Man* and *The Stars My Destination*. Then he
turned to other fields of writing, and no science-
fiction editor has been able to lure him back.
The fierce and funny story here shows Bester
at the peak of his form: inventive, sardonic,
compassionate, altogether brilliant.

This one wasn't the last war or a war to end war. They
called it the War for the American Dream. General Carpenter struck that note and sounded it constantly.

There are fighting generals (vital to an army), political
generals (vital to an administration), and public relations
generals (vital to a war). General Carpenter was a master
of public relations. Forthright and Four-square, he had
ideals as high and as understandable as the mottoes on
money. In the mind of America he *was* the army, the administration, the nation's shield and sword and stout right
arm. His ideal was the American Dream.

"We are not fighting for money, for power, or for world
domination," General Carpenter announced at the Press
Association dinner.

"We are fighting solely for the American Dream," he
said to the 137th Congress.

"Our aim is not aggression or the reduction of nations

156

to slavery," he said at the West Point Annual Officer's Dinner.

"We are fighting for the meaning of civilization," he told the San Francisco Pioneers' Club.

"We are struggling for the ideal of civilization; for culture, for poetry, for the Only Things Worth Preserving," he said at the Chicago Wheat Pit Festival.

"This is a war for survival," he said. "We are not fighting for ourselves, but for our dreams; for the Better Things in Life which must not disappear from the face of the earth."

America fought. General Carpenter asked for one hundred million men. The army was given one hundred million men. General Carpenter asked for ten thousand H-bombs. Ten thousand H-bombs were delivered and dropped. The enemy also dropped ten thousand H-bombs and destroyed most of America's cities.

"We must dig in against the hordes of barbarism," General Carpenter said. "Give me a thousand engineers."

One thousand engineers were forthcoming, and a hundred cities were dug and hollowed out beneath the rubble.

"Give me five hundred sanitation experts, three hundred traffic managers, two hundred air-conditioning experts, one hundred city managers, one thousand communication chiefs, seven hundred personnel experts. . . ."

The list of General Carpenter's demand for technical experts was endless. America did not know how to supply them.

"We must become a nation of experts," General Carpenter informed the National Association of American Universities. "Every man and woman must be a specific tool for a specific job, hardened and sharpened by your training and education to win the fight for the American Dream."

"Our Dream," General Carpenter said at the Wall Street Bond Drive Breakfast, "is at one with the gentle Greeks of Athens, with the noble Romans of . . . er . . . Rome. It is a dream of the Better Things in Life. Of music and art and poetry and culture. Money is only a weapon to be used in the fight for this dream. Ambition is only a ladder to climb to this dream. Ability is only a tool to shape this dream."

Wall Street applauded. General Carpenter asked for one hundred and fifty billion dollars, fifteen hundred ambitious dollar-a-year men, three thousand able experts in mineralogy, petrology, mass production, chemical warfare, and air-traffic time study. They were delivered. This country was in high gear. General Carpenter had only to press a button and an expert would be delivered.

In March of A.D. 2112 the war came to a climax and the American Dream was resolved, not on any one of the seven fronts where millions of men were locked in bitter combat, not in any of the staff headquarters or any of the capitals of the warring nations, not in any of the production centers spewing forth arms and supplies, but in Ward T of the United States Army Hospital buried three hundred feet below what had once been St. Albans, New York.

Ward T was something of a mystery at St. Albans. Like any army hospital, St. Albans was organized with specific wards reserved for specific injuries. All right-arm amputees were gathered in one ward, all left-arm amputees in another. Radiation burns, head injuries, eviscerations, secondary gamma poisonings and so on were each assigned their specific location in the hospital organization. The Army Medical Corps had designated nineteen classes of combat injury which included every possible kind of damage to brain and tissue. These used up letters A to S. What, then, was in Ward T?

No one knew. The doors were double locked. No visitors were permitted to enter. No patients were permitted to leave. Physicians were seen to arrive and depart. Their perplexed expressions stimulated the wildest speculations but revealed nothing. The nurses who ministered to Ward T were questioned eagerly but they were closemouthed.

There were dribs and drabs of information, unsatisfying and self-contradictory. A charwoman asserted that she had been in to clean up and there had been no one in the ward. Absolutely no one. Just two dozen beds and nothing else. Had the beds been slept in? Yes. They were rumpled, some of them. Were there signs of the ward being in use? Oh, yes. Personal things on the tables and so on. But dusty, kind of. Like they hadn't been used in a long time.

Public opinion decided it was a ghost ward. For spooks only.

But a night orderly reported passing the locked ward and hearing singing from within. What kind of singing? Foreign language, like. What language? The orderly couldn't say. Some of the words sounded like . . . well, like: Cow dee on us eager tour. . . .

Public opinion started to run a fever and decided it was an alien ward. For spies only.

St. Albans enlisted the help of the kitchen staff and checked the food trays. Twenty-four trays went into Ward T three times a day. Twenty-four came out. Sometimes the returning trays were emptied. Most times they were untouched.

Public opinion built up pressure and decided that Ward T was a racket. It was an informal club for goldbricks and staff grafters who caroused within. Cow dee on us eager tour indeed!

For gossip, a hospital can put a small-town sewing circle to shame with ease, but sick people are easily goaded into passion by trivia. It took just three months for idle speculation to turn into downright fury. In January, 2112, St. Albans was a sound, well-run hospital. By March, 2112, St. Albans was in a ferment, and the psychological unrest found its way into the official records. The percentage of recoveries fell off. Malingering set in. Petty infractions increased. Mutinies flared. There was a staff shake-up. It did no good. Ward T was inciting the patients to riot. There was another shake-up, and another, and still the unrest fumed.

The news finally reached General Carpenter's desk through official channels.

"In our fight for the American Dream," he said, "we must not ignore those who have already given of themselves. Send me a Hospital Administration expert."

The expert was delivered. He could do nothing to heal St. Albans. General Carpenter read the reports and broke him.

"Pity," said General Carpenter, "is the first ingredient of civilization. Send me a Surgeon General."

A Surgeon General was delivered. He could not break the fury of St. Albans, and General Carpenter broke him. But by this time Ward T was being mentioned in the dispatches.

"Send me," General Carpenter said, "the expert in charge of Ward T."

St. Albans sent a doctor, Captain Edsel Dimmock. He was a stout young man, already bald, only three years out of medical school but with a fine record as an expert in psychotherapy. General Carpenter liked experts. He liked Dimmock. Dimmock adored the general as the spokesman for a culture which he had been too specially trained to seek up to now, but which he hoped to enjoy after the war was won.

"Now look here, Dimmock," General Carpenter began. "We're all of us tools, today—sharpened and hardened to do a specific job. You know our motto: A job for everyone and everyone on the job. Somebody's not on the job at Ward T, and we've got to kick him out. Now, in the first place what the hell is Ward T?"

Dimmock stuttered and fumbled. Finally he explained

that it was a special ward set up for special combat cases. Shock cases.

"Then you do have patients in the ward?"

"Yes, sir. Ten women and fourteen men."

Carpenter brandished a sheaf of reports. "Says here the St. Albans patients claim nobody's in Ward T."

Dimmock was shocked. That was untrue, he assured the general.

"All right, Dimmock. So you've got your twenty-four crocks in there. Their job's to get well. Your job's to cure them. What the hell's upsetting the hospital about that?"

"W-well, sir. Perhaps it's because we keep them locked up."

"You keep Ward T locked?"

"Yes, sir."

"Why?"

"To keep the patients in, General Carpenter."

"Keep 'em in? What d'you mean? Are they trying to get out? They violent, or something?"

"No, sir. Not violent."

"Dimmock, I don't like your attitude. You're acting damned sneaky and evasive. And I'll tell you something else I don't like. That T classification. I checked with a Filing Expert from the Medical Corps, and there is no T classification. What the hell are you up to at St. Albans?"

"W-well, sir. . . . We invented the T classification. It . . . they . . . they're rather special cases, sir. We don't know what to do about them or how to handle them. W-we've been trying to keep it quiet until we've worked out a modus operandi, but it's brand-new, General Carpenter. Brand-new!" Here the expert in Dimmock triumphed over discipline. "It's sensational. It'll make medical history, by God! It's the biggest damned thing ever."

"What is it, Dimmock? Be specific."

"Well, sir, they're shock cases. Blanked out. Almost catatonic. Very little respiration. Slow pulse. No response."

"I've seen thousands of shock cases like that," Carpenter grunted. "What's so unusual?"

"Yes, sir. So far it sounds like the standard Q or R classification. But here's something unusual. They don't eat, and they don't sleep."

"Never?"

"Some of them never."

"Then why don't they die?"

"We don't know. The metabolism cycle's broken, but only on the anabolism side. Catabolism continues. In other words, sir, they're eliminating waste products, but they're not taking anything in. They're eliminating fatigue poisons and rebuilding worn tissue, but without sleep. God knows how. It's fantastic."

"That's why you've got them locked up? Mean to say . . . d'you suspect them of stealing food and cat naps somewhere else?"

"N-no, sir." Dimmock looked shamefaced. "I don't know how to tell you this, General Carpenter. I . . . we lock them up because of the real mystery. They . . . well, they disappear."

"They what?"

"They disappear, sir. Vanish. Right before your eyes."

"The hell you say."

"I do say, sir. They'll be sitting on a bed or standing around. One minute you see them; the next minute you don't. Sometimes there's two dozen in Ward T. Other times none. They disappear and reappear without rhyme or reason. That's why we've got the ward locked, General Carpenter. In the entire history of combat and combat injury there's never been a case like this before. We don't know how to handle it."

"Bring me three of those cases," General Carpenter said.

Nathan Riley ate french toast, eggs benedict, consumed two quarts of brown ale, smoked a John Drew, belched

delicately, and arose from the breakfast table. He nodded
quietly to Gentleman Jim Corbett, who broke off his conversation with Diamond Jim Brady to intercept him on the
way to the cashier's desk.

"Who do you like for the pennant this year, Nat?" Gentleman Jim inquired.

"The Dodgers," Nathan Riley answered.

"They've got no pitching."

"They've got Snider and Furillo and Campanella. They'll
take the pennant this year, Jim. I'll bet they take it earlier
than any team ever did. By September thirteenth. Make
a note. See if I'm right."

"You're always right, Nat," Corbett said.

Riley smiled, paid his check, sauntered out into the
street, and caught a horsecar bound for Madison Square
Garden. He got off at the corner of Fiftieth and Eighth
Avenue and walked upstairs to a handbook office over a
radio repair shop. The bookie glanced at him, produced an
envelope, and counted out fifteen thousand dollars.

"Rocky Marciano by a TKO over Roland La Starza in
the eleventh," he said. "How the hell do you call them so
accurate, Nat?"

"That's the way I make a living," Riley smiled. "Are
you making book on the elections?"

"Eisenhower twelve to five. Stevenson——"

"Never mind Adlai." Riley placed twenty thousand dollars on the counter. "I'm backing Ike. Get this down for
me."

He left the handbook office and went to his suite in the
Waldorf where a tall, thin young man was waiting for him
anxiously.

"Oh, yes," Nathan Riley said. "You're Ford, aren't you?
Harold Ford?"

"Henry Ford, Mr. Riley."

"And you need financing for that machine in your bicycle
shop. What's it called?"

"I call it an Ipsimobile, Mr. Riley."

"Hmmm. Can't say I like that name. Why not call it an automobile?"

"That's a wonderful suggestion, Mr. Riley. I'll certainly take it."

"I like you, Henry. You're young, eager, adaptable. I believe in your future, and I believe in your automobile. I'll invest two hundred thousand dollars in your company."

Riley wrote a check and ushered Henry Ford out. He glanced at his watch and suddenly felt impelled to go back and look around for a moment. He entered his bedroom, undressed, put on a gray shirt and gray slacks. Across the pocket of the shirt were large blue letters: U.S.A.H.

He locked the bedroom door and disappeared.

He reappeared in Ward T of the United States Army Hospital in St. Albans, standing alongside his bed which was one of twenty-four lining the walls of a long, light steel barracks. Before he could draw another breath, he was seized by three pairs of hands. Before he could struggle, he was shot by a pneumatic syringe and poleaxed by 1½ cc of sodium thiomorphate.

"We've got one," someone said.

"Hang around," someone else answered. "General Carpenter said he wanted three."

After Marcus Junius Brutus left her bed, Lela Machan clapped her hands. Her slave women entered the chamber and prepared her bath. She bathed, dressed, scented herself, and breakfasted on Smyrna figs, Rose oranges, and a flagon of Lachryma Christi. Then she smoked a cigarette and ordered her litter.

The gates of her house were crowded as usual by adoring hordes from the Twentieth Legion. Two centurions removed her chair-bearers from the poles of the litter and bore her on their stout shoulders. Lela Machan smiled. A young man in a sapphire-blue cloak thrust through the mob and ran toward her. A knife flashed in his hand. Lela braced herself to meet death bravely.

"Lady!" he cried. "Lady Lela!"

He slashed his left arm with the knife and let the crimson blood stain her robe.

"This blood of mine is the least I have to give you," he cried.

Lela touched his forehead gently.

"Silly boy," she murmured. "Why?"

"For love of you, my lady."

"You will be admitted tonight at nine," Lela whispered. He stared at her until she laughed. "I promise you. What is your name, pretty boy?"

"Ben Hur."

"Tonight at nine, Ben Hur."

The litter moved on. Outside the forum, Julius Caesar passed in hot argument with Marcus Antonius Antony. When he saw the litter he motioned sharply to the centurions, who stopped at once. Caesar swept back the curtains and stared at Lela, who regarded him languidly. Caesar's face twitched.

"Why?" he asked hoarsely. "I have begged, pleaded, bribed, wept, and all without forgiveness. Why, Lela? Why?"

"Do you remember Boadicea?" Lela murmured.

"Boadicea? Queen of the Britons? Good God, Lela, what can she mean to our love? I did not love Boadicea. I merely defeated her in battle."

"And killed her, Caesar."

"She poisoned herself, Lela."

"She was my mother, Caesar!" Suddenly Lela pointed her finger at Caesar. "Murderer. You will be punished. Beware the Ides of March, Caesar!"

Caesar recoiled in horror. The mob of admirers that had gathered around Lela uttered a shout of approval. Amidst a rain of rose petals and violets she continued on her way across the Forum to the Temple of the Vestal Virgins, where she abandoned her adoring suitors and entered the sacred temple.

Before the altar she genuflected, intoned a prayer, dropped a pinch of incense on the altar flame, and disrobed. She examined her beautiful body reflected in a silver mirror, then experienced a momentary twinge of homesickness. She put on a gray blouse and a gray pair of slacks. Across the pocket of the blouse was lettered U.S.A.H.

She smiled once at the altar and disappeared.

She reappeared in Ward T of the United States Army Hospital where she was instantly felled by 1½ cc of sodium thiomorphate injected subcutaneously by a pneumatic syringe.

"That's two," somebody said.

"One more to go."

George Hanmer paused dramatically and stared around . . . at the opposition benches, at the Speaker on the woolsack, at the silver mace on a crimson cushion before the Speaker's chair. The entire House of Parliament, hypnotized by Hanmer's fiery oratory, waited breathlessly for him to continue.

"I can say no more," Hanmer said at last. His voice was choked with emotion. His face was blanched and grim. "I will fight for this bill at the beachheads. I will fight in the cities, the towns, the fields, and the hamlets. I will fight for this bill to the death and, God willing, I will fight for it after death. Whether this be a challenge or a prayer, let the consciences of the right honorable gentlemen determine; but of one thing I am sure and determined: England must own the Suez Canal."

Hanmer sat down. The house exploded. Through the cheering and applause he made his way out into the division lobby where Gladstone, Canning, and Peel stopped him to shake his hand. Lord Palmerston eyed him coldly, but Pam was shouldered aside by Disraeli who limped up, all enthusiasm, all admiration.

"We'll have a bite at Tattersall's," Dizzy said. "My car's waiting."

Lady Beaconfield was in the Rolls Royce outside the Houses of Parliament. She pinned a primrose on Dizzy's lapel and patted Hanmer's cheek affectionately.

"You've come a long way from the schoolboy who used to bully Dizzy, Georgie," she said.

Hanmer laughed. Dizzy sang: *"Gaudeamus igitur . . ."* and Hanmer chanted the ancient scholastic song until they reached Tattersall's. There Dizzy ordered Guinness and grilled bones while Hanmer went upstairs in the club to change.

For no reason at all he had the impulse to go back for a last look. Perhaps he hated to break with his past completely. He divested himself of his surtout, nankeen waistcoat, pepper and salt trousers, polished Hessians, and undergarments. He put on a gray shirt and gray trousers and disappeared.

He reappeared in Ward T of the St. Albans Hospital where he was rendered unconscious by 1½ cc of sodium thiomorphate.

"That's three," somebody said.

"Take 'em to Carpenter."

So there they sat in General Carpenter's office, PFC Nathan Riley, M/Sgt Lela Machan, and Corp/2 George Hanmer. They were in their hospital grays. They were torpid with sodium thiomorphate.

The office had been cleared, and it blazed with blinding light. Present were experts from Espionage, Counterespionage, Security, and Central Intelligence. When Captain Edsel Dimmock saw the steel-faced ruthless squad awaiting the patients and himself, he started. General Carpenter smiled grimly.

"Didn't occur to you that we mightn't buy your disappearance story, eh, Dimmock?"

"S-sir?"

"I'm an expert, too, Dimmock. I'll spell it out for you. The war's going badly. Very badly. There've been intelligence leaks. The St. Albans mess might point to you."

"B-but they do disappear, sir. I——"

"My experts want to talk to you and your patients about this disappearance act, Dimmock. They'll start with you."

The experts worked over Dimmock with preconscious softeners, id releases, and superego blocks. They tried every truth serum in the books and every form of physical and mental pressure. They brought Dimmock, squealing, to the breaking point three times, but there was nothing to break.

"Let him stew for now," Carpenter said. "Get on to the patients."

The experts appeared reluctant to apply pressure to the sick men and the woman.

"For God's sake, don't be squeamish," Carpenter raged. "We're fighting a war for civilization. We've got to protect our ideals no matter what the price. Get to it!"

The experts from Espionage, Counterespionage, Security, and Central Intelligence got to it. Like three candles, PFC Nathan Riley, M/Sgt Lela Machan, and Corp/2 George Hanmer snuffed out and disappeared. One moment they were seated in chairs surrounded by violence. The next moment they were not.

The experts gasped. General Carpenter did the handsome thing. He stalked to Dimmock. "Captain Dimmock, I apologize. Colonel Dimmock, you've been promoted for making an important discovery . . . only what the hell does it mean? We've got to check ourselves first."

Carpenter snapped up the intercom. "Get me a combat-shock expert and an alienist."

The two experts entered and were briefed. They examined the witnesses. They considered.

"You're all suffering from a mild case of shock," the combat-shock expert said. "War jitters."

"You mean we didn't see them disappear?"

The shock expert shook his head and glanced at the alienist who also shook his head.

"Mass illusion," the alienist said.

At that moment PFC Riley, M/Sgt Machan, and Corp/2 Hanmer reappeared. One moment they were a mass illusion; the next, they were back sitting in their chairs surrounded by confusion.

"Dope 'em again, Dimmock," Carpenter cried. "Give 'em a gallon." He snapped up his intercom. "I want every expert we've got. Emergency meeting in my office at once."

Thirty-seven experts, hardened and sharpened tools all, inspected the unconscious shock cases and discussed them for three hours. Certain facts were obvious: This must be a new fantastic syndrome brought on by the new and fantastic horrors of the war. As combat technique develops, the response of victims of this technique must also take new roads. For every action there is an equal and opposite reaction. Agreed.

This new syndrome must involve some aspects of teleportation . . . the power of mind over space. Evidently combat shock, while destroying certain known powers of the mind, must develop other latent powers hitherto unknown. Agreed.

Obviously, the patients must only be able to return to the point of departure; otherwise they would not continue to return to Ward T, nor would they have returned to General Carpenter's office. Agreed.

Obviously, the patients must be able to procure food and sleep wherever they go, since neither was required in Ward T. Agreed.

"One small point," Colonel Dimmock said. "They seem

to be returning to Ward T less frequently. In the beginning they would come and go every day or so. Now most of them stay away for weeks and hardly ever return."

"Never mind that," Carpenter said. "Where do they go?"

"Do they teleport behind the enemy lines?" someone asked. "There's those intelligence leaks."

"I want Intelligence to check," Carpenter snapped. "Is the enemy having similar difficulties with, say, prisoners of war who appear and disappear from their POW camps? They might be some of ours from Ward T."

"They might simply be going home," Colonel Dimmock suggested.

"I want Security to check," Carpenter ordered. "Cover the homelife and associations of every one of those twenty-four disappearers. Now . . . about our operations in Ward T. Colonel Dimmock has a plan."

"We'll set up six extra beds in Ward T," Edsel Dimmock explained. "We'll send in six experts to live there and observe. Information must be picked up indirectly from the patients. They're catatonic and nonresponsive when conscious and incapable of answering questions when drugged."

"Gentlemen," Carpenter summed it up. "This is the greatest potential weapon in the history of warfare. I don't have to tell you what it can mean to us to be able to teleport an entire army behind enemy lines. We can win the war for the American Dream in one day if we can win this secret hidden in those shattered minds. We must win!"

The experts hustled, Security checked, Intelligence probed. Six hardened and sharpened tools moved into Ward T in St. Albans Hospital and slowly got acquainted with the disappearing patients who appeared and departed less and less frequently. The tension increased.

Security was able to report that not one case of strange

appearance had taken place in America in the past year. Intelligence reported that the enemy did not seem to be having similar difficulties with their own shock cases or with POW's.

Carpenter fretted. "This is all brand-new. We've got no specialists to handle it. We've got to develop new tools." He snapped up his intercom. "Get me a college," he said.

They got him Yale.

"I want some experts in mind over matter. Develop them," Carpenter ordered. Yale at once introduced three graduate courses in Thaumaturgy, Extrasensory Perception, and Telekinesis.

The first break came when one of the Ward T experts requested the assistance of another expert. He wanted a Lapidary.

"What the hell for?" Carpenter wanted to know.

"He picked up a reference to a gem stone," Colonel Dimmock explained. "He can't relate it to anything in his experience. He's a personnel specialist."

"And he's not supposed to," Carpenter said approvingly. "A job for every man and every man on the job." He flipped up the intercom. "Get me a Lapidary."

An expert Lapidary was given leave of absence from the army arsenal and asked to identify a type of diamond called Jim Brady. He could not.

"We'll try it from another angle," Carpenter said. He snapped up his intercom. "Get me a Semanticist."

The Semanticist left his desk in the War Propaganda Department but could make nothing of the words "Jim Brady." They were names to him. No more. He suggested a Genealogist.

A Genealogist was given one day's leave from his post with the Un-American Ancestors Committee but could make nothing of the name Brady beyond the fact that it had been a common name in America for five hundred years. He suggested an Archaeologist.

An Archaeologist was released from the Cartography Division of Invasion Command and instantly identified the name Diamond Jim Brady. It was a historic personage who had been famous in the city of Little Old New York some time between Governor Peter Stuyvesant and Governor Fiorello La Guardia.

"Christ!" Carpenter marveled. "That's centuries ago. Where the hell did Nathan Riley get that? You'd better join the experts in Ward T and follow this up."

The Archaeologist followed it up, checked his references, and sent in his report. Carpenter read it and was stunned. He called an emergency meeting of his staff of experts.

"Gentlemen," he announced, "Ward T is something bigger than teleportation. Those shock patients are doing something far more incredible . . . far more meaningful. Gentlemen, they're traveling through time."

The staff rustled uncertainly. Carpenter nodded emphatically.

"Yes, gentlemen, time travel is here. It has not arrived the way we expected it . . . as a result of expert research by qualified specialists; it has come as a plague . . . an infection . . . a disease of the war . . . a result of combat injury to ordinary men. Before I continue, look through these reports for documentation."

The staff read the stenciled sheets. PFC Nathan Riley . . . disappearing into the early twentieth century in New York; M/Sgt Lela Machan . . . visiting the first century in Rome; Corp/2 George Hanmer . . . journeying into the nineteenth century in England. And all the rest of the twenty-four patients, escaping the turmoil and horrors of modern war in the twenty-second century by fleeing to Venice and the Doges, to Jamaica and the buccaneers, to China and the Han Dynasty, to Norway and Eric the Red, to any place and any time in the world.

"I needn't point out the colossal significance of this discovery," General Carpenter pointed out. "Think what it would mean to the war if we could send an army back in time a week or a month or a year. We could win the war before it started. We could protect our Dream—poetry and beauty and the fine culture of America—from barbarism without ever endangering it."

The staff tried to grapple with the problem of winning battles before they started.

"The situation is complicated by the fact that these men and women of Ward T are *non compos*. They may or may not know how they do what they do, but in any case they're incapable of communicating with the experts who could reduce this miracle to method. It's for us to find the key. They can't help us."

The hardened and sharpened specialists looked around uncertainly.

"We'll need experts," General Carpenter said.

The staff relaxed. They were on familiar ground again.

"We'll need a Cerebral Mechanist, a Cyberneticist, a Psychiatrist, an Anatomist, an Archaeologist, and a first-rate Historian. They'll go into that ward, and they won't come out until their job is done. They must get the technique of time travel."

The first five experts were easy to draft from other war departments. All America was a tool chest of hardened and sharpened specialists. But there was trouble locating a first-class Historian until the Federal Penitentiary cooperated with the army and released Dr. Bradley Scrim from his twenty years at hard labor. Dr. Scrim was acid and jagged. He had held the chair of Philosophic History at a western university until he spoke his mind about the war for the American Dream. That got him the twenty years hard.

Scrim was still intransigent but induced to play ball by the intriguing problem of Ward T.

"But I'm not an expert," he snapped. "In this benighted

nation of experts, I'm the last singing grasshopper in the ant heap."

Carpenter snapped up the intercom. "Get me an Entomologist," he said.

"Don't bother," Scrim said. "I'll translate. You're a nest of ants . . . all working and toiling and specializing. For what?"

"To preserve the American Dream," Carpenter answered hotly. "We're fighting for poetry and culture and education and the Finer Things in Life."

"You're fighting to preserve me," Scrim said. "That's what I've devoted my life to. And what do you do with me? Put me in jail."

"You were convicted of enemy sympathizing and fellow-traveling," Carpenter said.

"I was convicted of believing in the American Dream," Scrim said. "Which is another way of saying I had a mind of my own."

Scrim was also intransigent in Ward T. He stayed one night, enjoyed three good meals, read the reports, threw them down, and began hollering to be let out.

"There's a job for everyone, and everyone must be on the job," Colonel Dimmock told him. "You don't come out until you've got the secret of time travel."

"There's no secret I can get," Scrim said.

"Do they travel in time?"

"Yes and no."

"The answer has to be one or the other. Not both. You're evading the——"

"Look," Scrim interrupted wearily. "What are you an expert in?"

"Psychotherapy."

"Then how the hell can you understand what I'm talking about? This is a philosophic concept. I tell you there's no secret here that the army can use. There's no secret any group can use. It's a secret for individuals only."

"I don't understand you."

"I didn't think you would. Take me to Carpenter."

They took Scrim to Carpenter's office where he grinned at the general malignantly, looking for all the world like a redheaded, underfed devil.

"I'll need ten minutes," Scrim said. "Can you spare them out of your toolbox?"

Carpenter nodded.

"Now listen carefully. I'm going to give you all the clues to something vast, so strange, so new, that it will need all your fine edge to cut into it."

Carpenter looked expectant.

"Nathan Riley goes back in time to the early twentieth century. There he lives the life of his fondest dreams. He's a big-time gambler, the friend of Diamond Jim Brady and others. He wins money betting on events because he always knows the outcome in advance. He won money betting on Eisenhower to win an election. He won money betting on a prizefighter named Marciano to beat another prizefighter named La Starza. He made money investing in an auto-mobile company owned by Henry Ford. There are the clues. They mean anything to you?"

"Not without a Sociological Analyst," Carpenter answered. He reached for the intercom.

"Don't bother. I'll explain. Let's try some more clues. Lela Machan, for example. She escapes into the Roman empire where she lives the life of her dreams as a *femme fatale*. Every man loves her. Julius Caesar, Brutus, the entire Twentieth Legion, a man named Ben Hur. Do you see the fallacy?"

"No."

"She also smokes cigarettes."

"Well?" Carpenter asked after a pause.

"I continue," Scrim said. "George escapes into England of the nineteenth century where he's a member of parlia-ment and the friend of Gladstone, Canning, and Disraeli,

who takes him riding in his Rolls Royce. Do you know what
a Rolls Royce is?"

"No."

"It was the name of an automobile."

"So?"

"You don't understand yet?"

"No."

Scrim paced the floor in exaltation. "Carpenter, this is a
bigger discovery than teleportation or time travel. This
can be the salvation of man. I don't think I'm exaggerating.
Those two dozen shock victims in Ward T have been H-
bombed into something so gigantic that it's no wonder your
specialists and experts can't understand it."

"What the hell's bigger than time travel, Scrim?"

"Listen to this, Carpenter. Eisenhower did not run for
office until the middle of the twentieth century. Nathan
Riley could not have been a friend of Diamond Jim
Brady's and bet on Eisenhower to win an election . . . not
simultaneously. Brady was dead a quarter of a century before Ike was President. Marciano defeated La Starza fifty
years after Henry Ford started his automobile company.
Nathan Riley's time-traveling is full of similar anachronisms."

Carpenter looked puzzled.

"Lela Machan could not have had Ben Hur for a lover.
Ben Hur never existed in Rome. He never existed at all. He
was a character in a novel. She couldn't have smoked. They
didn't have tobacco then. You see? More anachronisms.
Disraeli could never have taken George Hanmer for a ride
in a Rolls Royce because automobiles weren't invented
until long after Disraeli's death."

"The hell you say," Carpenter exclaimed. "You mean
they're all lying?"

"No. Don't forget, they don't need sleep. They don't
need food. They're not lying. They're going back in time
all right. They're eating and sleeping back there."

"But you just said their stories don't stand up. They're full of anachronisms."

"Because they travel back into a time of their own imagination. Nathan Riley has his own picture of what America was like in the early twentieth century. It's faulty and anachronistic because he's no scholar; but it's real for him. He can live there. The same is true for the others."

Carpenter goggled.

"The concept is almost beyond understanding. These people have discovered how to turn dreams into reality. They know how to enter their dream realities. They can stay there, live there, perhaps forever. My God, Carpenter, *this* is your American Dream. It's miracle-working, immortality, God-like creation, mind over matter. . . . It must be explored. It must be studied. It must be given to the world."

"Can you do it, Scrim?"

"No, I cannot. I'm a historian. I'm noncreative, so it's beyond me. You need a poet . . . a man who understands the creation of dreams. From creating dreams on paper or canvas it oughtn't to be too difficult to take the step to creating dreams in actuality."

"A poet? Are you serious?"

"Certainly I'm serious. Don't you know what a poet is? You've been telling us for five years that this war is being fought to save the poets."

"Don't be facetious, Scrim, I——"

"Send a poet into Ward T. He'll learn how they do it. He's the only man who can. A poet is half doing it anyway. Once he learns, he can teach your psychologists and anatomists. Then they can teach us; but the poet is the only man who can interpret between those shock cases and your experts."

"I believe you're right, Scrim."

"Then don't delay, Carpenter. Those patients are returning to this world less and less frequently. We've got to get

at that secret before they disappear forever. Send a pc
to Ward T."

Carpenter snapped up his intercom. "Send me a poe
he said.

He waited and waited . . . and waited . . . while Ameri
sorted feverishly through its two hundred and ninety m
lions of hardened and sharpened experts, its specializ
tools to defend the American Dream of beauty and poet
and the Better Things in Life. He waited for them to fir
a poet, not understanding the endless delay, the fruitle
search; not understanding why Bradley Scrim laugh
and laughed and laughed at this final, fatal disappearanc

Popular and bestselling
SCIENCE FICTION
FUTURISTIC · HORROR

PARADISE IS NOT ENOUGH, by Michael Elder. First American reprint of a British science fiction bestseller. The technology of two hundred years from now has turned the earth into utopia, but perfection is, for human beings, perhaps the greatest imperfection of all. The idle population has nothing to do but enjoy itself, and pleasure has become a big bore. The last employed people are the actors, who provide the entertainment for the never-ending canned television shows. When even this is threatened by automation, all hell breaks loose—in paradise!

P00034-0—95¢

THE OTHER SIDE OF THE CLOCK, collected by Philip Van Doren Stern. A collection of superb science fiction short stories. Included are such masters as Robert Heinlein, J. B. Priestly, H. G. Wells. The collection includes twelve tales that take the reader both backward and forward in time, the unifying element that is central to the book. Because the span encompasses all of eternity, time passed and time to come, the authors have a wide spectrum in which to work, and give the book a marvelous pace and variety not often found in such collections.

P00036-7—95¢

THE ALIEN EARTH, by Michael Elder. Cut off from his mother ship by a sudden disaster, Trist-space pilot from a far-off planet—is isolated somewhere in deep space. Only one star is within range, and he manages to crash land on one of its planets. He needs help to make repairs before he can lift off for home, but the natives he encounters know nothing of modern science and cannot aid him. Instead they spend all their time fighting each other and people they call "Romans." Through the use of long-sleep pills, he wakens to an even stranger scene 3000 years later, where . . . ? An alarmingly perceptive, prophetic book.

P00043-X—95¢

TALES FROM THE UNKNOWN, by Kurt Singer. This is not only a collection presenting psychic testimony from among the most notable writers of our time, but a pilgrimage to those hidden shrines and altars where the unbelievable is man's doctrine of faith. Through Kurt Singer, a master of the macabre, the reader visits Haiti, to meet a sorceress as well as a priestess of Voodoo; to Russia, where an incredibly beautiful but bewitched emerald affected the history of that nation for three hundred years; to Tahiti, to witness the ritual firewalk; and, in New York City, where witchcraft and worship of the devil have been revived at the Satan Church. Guaranteed to chill, intrigue and entertain.

P00054-5—95¢

CIVIL WAR II, by Dan Britain. A frightening look at what may well be the future of the United States—when the government is confronted by a *coup* by the long-repressed blacks who are in control of the military apparatus of the nation. Mike Winston, a white government official in charge of the "towns" in which the Negroes are forced to live, uncovers the plot—but too late to forestall the inevitable. In the days that follow he is placed in a position where he can help to save the country, or destroy it! A book both exciting and prophetic—you won't be able to put it down until the last page. P00055-3—95¢

FIRST CONTACT, edited by Damon Knight. Here are ten masterpieces of science-fiction and fantasy dealing with man's first encounter with alien creatures from outer space. With all the benefits of our science and history we earthlings still seem to find it impossible to communicate effectively. What is to be expected when our people make contact with creatures or intelligences from other worlds? Perhaps the answers to our problems are to be found in these prophetic and exciting stories from the imaginations of such masters of the game as: Leinster, Sturgeon, Asimov, Henneberg, Kornbluth, Heinlein, and H. G. Wells.

P00062-6—95¢

BEYOND THE CURTAIN OF DARKNESS, edited by Peter Haining. This is probably the most representative selection of horror and fantasy stories ever to appear in an American paperback. All the giants of the genre are included: oldies like Poe, Hawthorne, Bierce and Lovecraft, and current favorites like Bradbury, Sturgeon, Asimov, Highsmith and Kuttner. And there's Harold Lawlor, Fred Brown, Bill Morrow, Mary Shelley, August Derleth, Joe Le Fanu, and many more. Here are axe murderers, blood-sucking creatures, monster-makers, devils and demons, vampires and vultures, and all the weird and nameless horrors loved by all. P00138-X—$1.25

NOWHERE ON EARTH, by Michael Elder. Here is superior science fiction with the threat of reality, for this is the odyssey of one very ordinary man, fighting for his family in a world in which rebellion, either in thought or deed, is not tolerated. His story is both engrossing and frightening—it is a story that is just around the corner from today. Roger Barclay is hunting for his wife and newborn daughter, who have disappeared from a maternity hospital. No one will answer his anguished questions, so he turns to an underground group, led by a mysterious revolutionary, for help. What he finds will surprise you.

P00157-6—95¢

SCIENTIFIC ASTROLOGY, by Sir John Manolesco. Finally, the inside truth about astrology! Here is a clear, authoritative and absorbing look at a very old subject, one that has long been fascinating to both fans and cynics. It is a most unique exploration of an influential force at work on all of our lives. Sir John's book gives outsiders an inside look; the whole truth about astrology: the information necessary to evaluate any given astrological source. **P00176-2—95¢**

DREAM-SCOPE, by Sydney Omarr. Here, from the man named "Outstanding Contributor to the Advancement of Astrology," is a revolutionary method of tapping the world of dreams, of viewing them both in the form of written words and pictures. DREAM-SCOPE allows each reader to embark upon adventures previously confined to the world of sleep. All the mysteries of dream interpretation are revealed, permitting the reader to "see" his dream as he never could before—but always wanted to. From cover to cover, DREAM-SCOPE is a dream of a book. **P00185-1—95¢**

FLIGHT TO TERROR, by Michael Elder. Seven people marooned on an enchanted planet! In this exciting sequel to *Nowhere on Earth*, a space crew from earth orbits Roker II—a beautiful, spell-binding planet. A group of experts leaves the ship to search for a small colony of people who have taken up residence there. As they fall towards the planet, the ship that they have left disappears and they quickly become the ones who are in need of rescue. Stranded on this strange planet, these seven survivors suddenly discover the frightening truth about what happened to the first colony. **P00219-X—95¢**

MIND OUT, by Diana Carter. A provocative novel about a far-out communal group. The "Cerebralists" are a group who entice young, alienated, often rather confused young people to join their strange cult. They are then forced to sign over all their property. But to whom? No one knows the leader. He communicates with his members through strange codes and supervises them by closed-circuit TV. There are strange, mind-bending initiation rites, which some do not survive and which leave others in a permanent childlike state. Giselle Baker is the child of a famous, but aging, French movie actress. She is induced to join the group by the first man she meets. What happens to her will frighten and fascinate you. A book no one will be able to put down. **P00220-3—95¢**

THIS IS YOUR ORDER FORM.
CLIP AND MAIL.

_____	P00034-0 PARADISE IS NOT ENOUGH, Michael Elder	.95
_____	P00036-7 THE OTHER SIDE OF THE CLOCK, Philip Van Doren Stern	.95
_____	P00043-X THE ALIEN EARTH, Michael Elder	.95
_____	P00054-5 TALES FROM THE UNKNOWN, Kurt Singer	.95
_____	P00055-3 CIVIL WAR II, Dan Britain	.95
_____	P00062-6 FIRST CONTACT, Damon Knight	.95
_____	P00138-X BEYOND THE CURTAIN OF DARKNESS, Peter Haining	1.25
_____	P00157-6 NOWHERE ON EARTH, Michael Elder	.95
_____	P00176-2 SCIENTIFIC ASTROLOGY, John Manolesco	.95
_____	P00185-1 DREAM-SCOPE, Sydney Omarr	.95
_____	P00219-X FLIGHT TO TERROR, Michael Elder	.95
_____	P00220-3 MIND OUT, Diana Carter	.95

TO ORDER

Please check the space next to the book/s you want, send this order form together with your check or money order, include the price of the book/s and 25¢ for handling and mailing. to:

PINNACLE BOOKS, INC.
P.O. Box 4347 / Grand Central Station
New York, N.Y. 10017

☐ CHECK HERE IF YOU WANT A FREE CATALOG.

I have enclosed $_____ check_____ or money order_____ as payment in full. No C.O.D.'s.

Name_____

Address_____

City_____ State_____ Zip_____
(Please allow time for delivery.)